DJ walked over to the window. There was the house across the street. He could feel it staring at him, the windows like great glass eyes that sensed his presence and seemed to track his every move. As he watched, a wispy ribbon of black smoke rose from the chimney. Just then a cold gust of wind blew sharply toward him, so strongly that he had to pull his telescope inside and close the window.

DJ shook his head, lowered the blinds, and fell back on his bed. As he slept, he dreamed that his room grew darker and darker as the shadow of Mr. Nebbercracker's house crept ominously across his floor. Extending itself toward DJ, the silent shadow also grew larger and larger, suddenly changing into a giant bony hand that seemed ready to pounce—

MONSTER HOUSE™

THERE GOES THE NEIGHBORHOOD . . .

MONSTER HOUSE ™

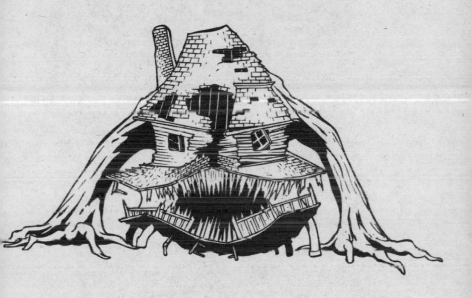

adapted by Tom Hughes
based on the screenplay by Dan Harmon & Rob Schrab and Pamela Pettler
Story by Dan Harmon & Rob Schrab

Simon Spotlight
New York   London   Toronto   Sydney

This book is a work of fiction. Any references to historical events, real people, or real locales are used fictitiously. Other names, characters, places, and incidents are the product of the author's imagination, and any resemblance to actual events or locales or persons, living or dead, is entirely coincidental.

SIMON SPOTLIGHT
An imprint of Simon & Schuster
Children's Publishing Division
1230 Avenue of the Americas, New York, New York 10020
Copyright © 2006 by Columbia Pictures Industries, Inc.
All Rights Reserved.
All rights reserved, including the right of reproduction in
whole or in part in any form.
SIMON SPOTLIGHT and colophon are registered trademarks
of Simon & Schuster, Inc.
Manufactured in the U.S.A.
First Edition
2 4 6 8 10 9 7 5 3 1
ISBN-13: 978-1-4169-1817-2
ISBN-10: 1-4169-1817-5

CHAPTER 1

On the afternoon before Halloween, in the town of Mayville, a little girl with pigtails was pedaling her Big Wheel furiously through the colorful fallen leaves that had blanketed the sidewalks and lawns of Oak Street. Zigging and zagging happily around big cracks in the pavement and the gnarled, exposed roots of trees lining the road, she skidded just a little too far and ended up on the edge of a well-kept front lawn.

Suddenly a strange moaning sound made the little girl look up. The pristine lawn belonged to a weathered clapboard house that gleamed in the sun. Above the perfectly centered front door, two perfectly placed windows seemed to glare down at her like eyes.

Then the girl heard a shriek and the front door flew open.

"Get off my lawn!" someone yelled.

It was old Mr. Nebbercracker. The little girl froze in terror.

"Trespasser!" he yelled furiously. "Do you want to be eaten alive?"

The girl abandoned her tricycle and backed away, shaking her head.

"Then get outta here!" Mr. Nebbercracker commanded.

After taking another step back, she turned and ran away as fast as she could. Mr. Nebbercracker stalked across the emerald grass, snatched the tricycle up in a gnarled hand, and snapped the front wheel off. "And stay away!"

"What's the matter with these kids?" he muttered as another strange moaning sound came from the house. "They never listen."

For a moment the moaning sound grew louder, and then it stopped. The elderly man turned and gazed angrily at the house across the street. After a moment, he muttered again, "They never listen," then stepped inside and slammed the door shut behind him.

CHAPTER 2

Twelve-year-old DJ Walters jumped back from his
telescope. He had seen the whole thing. The weirdest
part was that the old man, Mr. Nebbercracker, had
seemed to look straight at DJ, almost as if he knew he
was being watched.

"DJ!"

Ignoring the call, DJ turned from the window and
made a notation on a clipboard nearly covered with
numbers. He had written "Reaction Times" at the
top of the page. After what he'd just seen, he noted
"14 seconds" in his log. Then he added, "October 30.
Another tricycle."

"DJ!"

"I'm coming!" DJ yelled back, pulling on a jacket
and examining for the millionth time the photos
and drawings and diagrams that covered every square

inch of wall space in his room. They were all about the Nebbercracker house.

"DJ!"

DJ finally left his room. Exploding out of the house, he blinked in the bright, late-autumn sunshine as he met his parents in the front yard. "Mom, he did it again. He took another bike," he told his mother breathlessly.

DJ's mom glanced worriedly at his dad, who was trying to shove a giant plastic tooth into their station wagon. His parents were going to another one of their many dental conventions.

"Now, honey, we talked about this," she reminded her son. "You can't stay up in your room staring at an old man through a telescope."

"But there's something wrong with that house," DJ insisted.

DJ's dad gave up on the tooth for a moment. "You know, he's got a point," he said as he looked over at the Nebbercracker house. "There's nothing scarier than a well-manicured front lawn. Ups the bar for the rest of us, you know."

"I'm serious," DJ insisted, his voice suddenly cracking sharply.

"Hey, your voice sounds funny," said his mom.

His dad beamed. "Sounds like someone is growing

up. 'What's happening to my body?'—right, buddy?"

"Maybe you should come with us," his mom added quickly.

DJ's dad winked at his wife. "Oh, the boy's too busy," he whispered loudly. "He's got spying to do."

"I'm not spying," protested DJ. "I'm, I'm—"

Before DJ could finish, his dad stepped forward, holding the molar. "Well, that's okay, buddy. At your age I did exactly the same thing. Of course it was with binoculars and involved the lovely—"

Not wanting his wife to hear what he was saying, DJ's dad suddenly said loudly, "Dear, would you be an angel and help me bring out the incisor?"

He passed the molar to DJ and walked back into the house with his wife. DJ sighed and put the big tooth in the backseat of the car. He slammed the door, then turned to look at the creepy house across the street, which seemed to be staring at him.

A few moments later DJ's parents were back with another tooth. After placing it next to the molar, they settled into their car and revved the engine.

"Elizabeth will be here in a few hours," his mom called as they backed out of the driveway. "Remember, we'll be back tomorrow. If anything happens, call the police and hide in your closet!"

"He knows that," his dad said calmly, just as a chubby character clutching a basketball waddled full speed toward the car.

DJ's father slammed on the brakes.

"Sorry," the costumed figure apologized. "It's hard to see with the mask on."

DJ's dad rolled down his window and reached over to peel off the mask.

"Chowder!" he exclaimed, recognizing DJ's best friend.

"Happy Halloween," Chowder said sheepishly as DJ's dad shook his head and rolled up the window. Just as the car began to back down the driveway again, DJ's mom leaned over her husband and rolled down the window once more.

"We love you!" she called to DJ. "And that includes your dad!"

"That's right," his dad chimed in before pulling away.

CHAPTER 3

DJ groaned as he watched his parents drive off.

"Ah, cheer up," Chowder told him. "It's almost Halloween. In one day and three hours, it's C-A-N-D-Y time!"

Chowder jumped up and showed off his new basketball. "Check it out. I got a new ball." Faking a pass, he began to shoot some hoops at the basket over DJ's garage.

"Speaking of which," he continued, after taking a couple of shots, "have you decided yet? Skullzor or Cryptkeeper?"

"Chowder, I don't think I'm going trick-or-treating this year," DJ told him.

Chowder froze in the middle of an imaginary layup. The ball dropped from his hands.

"What?" he exclaimed. "C'mon, you're going

to break a six-year streak!"

"Six years of being jumped and egged," DJ replied, shooting a basket. "Maybe we're getting too grown-up."

Chowder whined at the idea.

"Speaking of which, you're not actually wearing the cape again, are you?" DJ asked accusingly.

Chowder balked. "What? I always wear the cape on Halloween. It's my thing. People expect it."

He grabbed the ball and made a drive for the basket.

"Three seconds on the clock," Chowder said in his announcer voice. "It's time for some in-your-face disgrace."

Hooking the ball hard, he hurled it into the air and turned to smirk at DJ. But DJ wasn't jealous. Instead, he waved his arms at the basket. "Watch out, Chowder!"

Chowder pivoted toward the basket. The ball ricocheted off the rim and hit him in the face. "Aaaaahhhhh! My face!" He collapsed on the driveway, clutching his nose with both hands.

"You okay?" asked DJ, rushing over to his friend.

Chowder moaned. "My nose is in my brain."

"Lemme see," DJ offered, kneeling next to Chowder.

Slowly Chowder removed his hands from his face. There was no blood, but DJ drew back in mock horror. "Oh, no!" he exclaimed.

"What?" demanded a terrified Chowder.

Putting on his most serious face, DJ pointed at him. "You're a dork," he joked, laughing.

Chowder ignored the comment. "Where's my ball?" he asked.

DJ, still laughing, looked around for the basketball. They both spotted it at the same time. "Oh, no," they moaned. The basketball was now sitting in the middle of Mr. Nebbercracker's lawn.

DJ and Chowder ran across the street and stopped short of the perfectly cut green grass.

"DJ, you're a grown-up now, " said Chowder. "You go get it."

DJ shook his head. "Your ball just landed on Nebbercracker's lawn," he told Chowder firmly. "It doesn't exist anymore."

But Chowder was not easily discouraged. "I paid twenty-eight dollars for that ball," he complained. "I raked ten yards and asked my mom for a dollar twenty-six times. I never worked that hard in my life."

DJ looked over at the quiet house. "Nebbercracker hasn't come out yet."

"So?" Chowder sniffed.

"So maybe he's sleeping." DJ looked around the front lawn. There was no sign of Mr. Nebbercracker. "Okay, I'll do it," he finally said.

He slowly put one foot on the lawn. The ball was right there, only a few feet away. He ran for it.

At that very moment, the front door was thrown open. DJ froze and stared at the door as an old man emerged from another part of the porch. "You!" said Mr. Nebbercracker, seeming to recognize DJ. Then he charged forward, screaming.

DJ barely had time to dodge as the old man lunged at him. He faked left and right, then ducked as Mr. Nebbercracker tried to grab him again. Suddenly DJ stopped short. He had wrenched out a piece of the well-kept lawn with his heel.

"I'm sorry," he frantically apologized.

"What have you done?" the old man yelled.

Turning to run, DJ started to cry for help but was cut off when Mr. Nebbercracker's hand closed on his shirt.

"You want to be a dead person?" Mr. Nebbercracker shrieked.

"No! I love life!" cried DJ.

His neighbor shook him again. "This is not a playground!" he declared.

DJ, still struggling, nodded quickly. "Got it! From

now on—," he began, but Mr. Nebbercracker's face had turned beet red, and every vein bulged in his thin neck. DJ felt himself being lifted off the ground by the collar of his T-shirt.

"This is my house," Mr. Nebbercracker roared desperately, raising DJ into the air. "Why can't you respect that? You of all people. Why can't you stay away from—"

The old man let out a loud groan and a cough. His grip on DJ loosened as his eyes bulged even more. With a final moan, Mr. Nebbercracker fell forward, toppling over DJ and pinning him to the ground.

"Uh-oh," Chowder whimpered from across the street.

Suddenly a cold gust of wind blew across the yard and the front door slammed shut.

CHAPTER 4

The sun was setting as DJ and Chowder watched paramedics lift Mr. Nebbercracker onto a gurney. As they pushed the gurney toward the ambulance, the grass seemed to grab for the wheels. No one noticed when one of the wheels broke off—and sank deep into the grass.

Drawn to a glint in the afternoon light, DJ found an old-fashioned key nestled in the lawn where Mr. Nebbercracker had fallen. For some reason, he slipped it into his pocket. The paramedics closed the ambulance doors and drove off.

"No siren," Chowder observed. "Never a good sign."

DJ shook his head. "I'm a murderer," he said in disbelief.

"No, you're not," Chowder contradicted him. "When it's an accident, they call it manslaughter."

DJ turned green. "I think I'm gonna throw up," he said, groaning.

Chowder shrugged, cast a final glance at Mr. Nebbercracker's house, and walked away. DJ watched him go and then dug out the old key he had found. Examining it in the last rays of the setting sun, he heard music blaring. And it wasn't coming from the house.

DJ looked up to see a very compact car pull into his driveway with the radio playing loudly. A twenty-something girl wearing a pastel cardigan and jeans hopped out.

"Hey there, buddy bear," she warbled happily at him. It was Elizabeth, the babysitter. "I saw an ambulance. Did I miss anything interesting?"

"Elizabeth, can I ask you something?" DJ asked when they were in the living room of his house.

Elizabeth plopped an overnight bag on the couch. "You sure can, cantaloupe," she twittered a little louder than necessary. "We are going to have the bestest time, I've got tons of neat activities planned!"

Noting her cheery voice, DJ figured Elizabeth thought his parents were still at home. "They already left," he informed her.

She glanced toward the stairs and then back at DJ. "They're not here?" she asked dubiously.

"No. And I need to talk to you . . . ," DJ began.

But Elizabeth was not listening as she pulled off her cardigan. Underneath was a black T-shirt sporting a skull and crossbones. "Okay, the usual deal," she said, her voice now significantly less pleasant. "Indoors by nine. In your room by eleven. Lights out, your call."

"Elizabeth," DJ persisted, using her real name to annoy her.

She glared at him. "And it's Zee," she corrected. "I control the TV, stereo, and phone. I don't do board games, Shrinky Dinks, or tuck-ins. I'm not your mother and I am not your friend."

"Don't talk to me like I'm a baby. I'm practically a grown-up!" DJ said defiantly. "I don't need you here, *Elizabeth*," he finished.

Zee responded by smiling in a way that made him nervous. Walking over to the credenza, she casually knocked over a potted plant, smashing it to pieces.

"Gosh, DJ," she said, faking a shocked tone. "Why did you break that?"

"But I didn't—," protested DJ.

Zee cut him off. "Who are they gonna believe?" she demanded.

DJ wanted to argue, but he knew he was beaten. He dragged himself upstairs as Zee put on loud rock music and looked through his parents' stuff.

Up in his room, he fished out the strange key he had found on his neighbor's front lawn. He examined it closely, hoping it might reveal something mysterious. But it just looked like it was an ordinary key.

Setting it down on his desk next to his journals and Polaroids, DJ walked over to the window. There was the house across the street. He could feel it staring at him, the windows like great glass eyes that sensed his presence and seemed to track his every move. As he watched, a wispy ribbon of black smoke rose from the chimney. Just then a cold gust of wind blew sharply toward him, so strongly that he had to pull his telescope inside and close the window.

DJ shook his head, lowered the blinds, and fell back on his bed. Reaching down, he pulled out an old stuffed animal. He had never been able to bring himself to get rid of good old Bunny. Smoothing down some of its fur, DJ gave it a hug and then quickly fell asleep.

As he slept, he dreamed that his room grew darker and darker as the shadow of Mr. Nebbercracker's house crept ominously across his floor. Extending itself toward DJ, the silent shadow also grew larger and larger, suddenly changing into a giant bony hand that seemed ready to pounce—

DJ shot out of bed to the sound of his phone ringing.

What a nightmare! That house—and strange Mr. Nebbercracker. He winced as he remembered the old man falling on top of him. He glanced at the illuminated numbers of his digital clock, shining in the darkness of his room. It was 11:14 p.m.

Rolling over to pick up the phone, DJ said, "Hello?"

When he heard a strange whispering sound on the other end, he hung up. A second later the phone rang again. DJ picked it up and heard the whispering once more.

"So funny," DJ said sarcastically, stabbing at the buttons on the phone. He punched *69. "Let's see how you like it." It had to be Chowder playing one of his dumb jokes, he thought.

The line rang. But he also heard the muffled ring of another phone, a barely audible ring. There was a ring coming from his receiver, but where was the other one coming from?

He looked around until he had it pinpointed. The ringing was coming from across the street—from a window in Mr. Nebbercracker's house!

Pulling up the shade and opening his window, DJ now heard it clearly. Shaking his head in disbelief, he hung up. When he dialed again, there could be no doubt. He had called Mr. Nebbercracker's house! And that meant that someone at that house had—

Letting the phone fall to his side, DJ backed away from the window, just as a pair of hands grabbed him in the dark.

"Aaaahhhhhhh!" he screamed. He spun around and looked into the eyes of a hideous creature glaring down at him.

CHAPTER 5

"Happy Halloween, doofus," the creature sneered in a gravelly voice as it pulled off Chowder's Halloween mask. It was an older rocker dude with long, stringy hair wearing a ripped denim jacket. He grinned stupidly down at DJ and started laughing.

Zee appeared in the room behind them. "Nice one, Bones!" she said, laughing as well.

Bones? thought DJ.

"Look at his face!" Bones said. "Oh, that's funny."

Stomping past him, DJ confronted Zee. "Who is this guy?" he asked. "You're not supposed to have friends over."

"This is Bones. He's in a band," Zee replied in a matter-of-fact tone. Then she backed DJ up against the wall with a pointed finger. "And let's not open up the rule book, since you're up way past your bedtime."

But DJ was barely listening. Now that the shock had worn off, he could still hear the faint ringing of the phone across the street.

"This is different," he insisted, holding the phone up to her ear and pointing out the window. "Listen."

Zee glanced out the window and nodded, looking at the phone. "You called the neighbors," she said. "Good for you." Taking the phone from him, she hung it up and then closed the window.

"I used star sixty-nine," DJ said. In a whisper he added, "He called me."

"Who called you?" Zee asked.

"Nebbercracker," DJ said ominously. "And P.S., he died today."

"You lie," Bones said.

"Do not. He died, and now I'm getting phone calls from his house!"

Still giggling, Bones teased, "A phone call. From beyond the grave."

He and Zee exchanged a glance, and they both moved toward DJ. "Ooooooohhh," they said, waving their hands in front of them like zombies.

DJ still tried to convince them. "You guys, I'm serious."

Bones just laughed harder. "Oh, he's serious," he said, walking over to the bed and scooping up Bunny. He waved it in the air. "Did you know he was serious?" he said to the stuffed animal.

"C'mon, give her back," DJ pleaded.

"Oh, her?" Bones laughed and began to kiss Bunny on the lips.

"C'mon, that's gross!" DJ yelled, trying to pull Bunny from him.

"Wait, hold on—I think she's having trouble breathing!" Bones taunted. "She might have something in her throat!" Bones began to rip the stuffing from the toy.

"No, don't!" DJ screamed.

"Bones!" Zee yelled. "That's enough! Downstairs. Now!"

"Sorry, kid. Can't play anymore," Bones said, smirking at DJ before tossing Bunny to the floor and slouching out of the room.

Zee slinked out after Bones. "You are so funny," she said to Bones before closing the door.

DJ could hear the two of them laughing as they went down the stairs. He picked Bunny up off the floor, then turned to the window. Peeking through the blinds, he surveyed the supposedly empty Nebbercracker house. It looked quiet. Then a shade on one of the windows snapped open—just like an eyelid!

DJ jumped back in fright and huddled against the wall next to the window. His heart was beating a mile a minute and he was shaking. After a while he forced himself to look out again and saw that the shade was drawn. But wait—was it . . . moving?

He backed away from the window. "Stop doing this," he whispered to himself as he reached for the phone. This time he knew exactly who he was calling.

"Homicide," Chowder said when he answered the phone.

"Chowder, where are your parents?" DJ asked.

"My dad's at the pharmacy, and my mom is at the movies with her personal trainer."

"Meet me at the danger zone. Now," DJ told him.

Talking on the couch in the living room, Bones and Zee didn't even notice DJ sneak down the stairs.

"Bones, I saw an ambulance up here today," Zee said as DJ tiptoed behind them and slipped quickly out the door.

Bones was not impressed. "So?"

"So?" Zee said. "Maybe Nebbercracker really did die."

Bones grinned at her, a malicious glint showing in his eyes. "We should be so lucky," he said. "The guy's evil."

"He's just a crotchety old dude," she countered.

Bones raised his eyebrows and leaned forward. "Oh, yeah?" he whispered, pausing dramatically before continuing. "When I was ten years old, I had a kite. An awesome kite."

Zee waited for him to tell his story.

"I could fly it so high you couldn't see it," Bones continued, gazing at the ceiling, pretending to be searching for the kite in a blue sky from years and years before. In his mind, that's what he was doing, running across bright green grass as fast as his little legs could go, his kite, shining red in the sun, rising higher and higher into the sky, free—as the string whizzed through his fingers. Soon the kite was just an animated crimson dot gliding and soaring among the clouds, tied to the earth and to Bones by nothing more than an almost invisible cotton string. As Bones told her the story, Zee felt like she could almost see him: little, innocent Bones in his grade-school uniform, flying his beloved red kite.

"One day," Bones said suddenly, "it crashed down." The glazed, happy look left his face. He remembered watching his kite jerk left and right.

No matter how he pulled and yanked on the string, the red dot in the sky grew and grew as his kite plummeted back to Earth and disappeared behind distant rooftops.

"I followed the string," he told her, sighing, remembering how lonely he'd felt as he held the slack string in his hand and began to walk. "And it ended right across the street . . . there."

Pausing to let that image sink in, he looked deeply into Zee's eyes, then added, "Right at the edge of his lawn."

Zee was now caught up in the story. "What happened?" she asked breathlessly.

Bones nodded, falling back away from Zee, against the cushions. "He took it, of course," he told her, getting angry at the memory. "He takes whatever lands on his lawn. But I saw it. My beautiful kite was right there on his stupid lawn. The tail was gone and one of the braces was broken, but I could've fixed it. I could've flown it again. I was just happy to have found my kite. As soon as I saw it, I started running."

Bones grew more animated and his words came out in a rush. "But he got there first. I thought he was going to kill me. He screamed at me! Asked me if I wanted to die! I begged him to give me my kite back, but he just told me to go away and never come back or I would get killed. Then he took my kite. Snatched it nearly out of my hands and went back to his front porch."

"Poor Bones," said Zee, stroking his long, greasy hair. "Did you ever see your kite again?"

"Naw-aw," Bones responded, shaking his head. "And I hid out and watched that house all night just to see if I could break in and get it back or . . . or something."

"Mr. Nebbercracker really is awful," Zee said sympathetically.

"But that's not the point," Bones said quickly, a strange, frightened gleam in his eyes. "The point is that I saw him talking to his house. And kissing it." He puckered his lips. "And besides," Bones added, "everyone knows what he did to his wife."

"What did he do to her?" asked Zee.

"He ate her!" yelled Bones, lunging at her and laughing. Zee screamed when he fell on her. Then he grunted loudly as she jabbed him with her knee.

"Bones, I'm so sick of you!" Zee exclaimed. "You have no respect for women!"

Bones was surprised. "What do you mean?" he asked.

Two seconds later the front door of the Walters' house slammed in his face.

"Fine!" Bones yelled at the door. He pulled a bottle out of his back pocket and sipped at it. Stepping off the porch and starting down the street, he stopped and glanced up at the Nebbercracker house, shining eerily in the moonlight.

"What are you looking at?" he asked it defiantly.

The house just stood there.

Walking closer to the edge of the Nebbercracker lawn, Bones smiled and tossed his bottle onto the grass, leaping back at the same time. He started to dance back and forth, like a boxer. "Yeah," he taunted. "C'mon. You like that?"

Growing braver by the second, he ran right up to the edge of the lawn and stomped on it, then quickly jumped back.

When nothing happened, Bones marched back onto the lawn and stood there. A triumphant smile slowly spread across his scruffy face. "You really are dead, aren't you?" he whispered, glancing around the deserted street. Taking two more steps forward, he waved his arms at the dark, empty house.

"I'm on your lawn, Nebbercracker," he teased. "What are you gonna do about it?"

Giggling, Bones began to stomp around in a small circle, crushing the tender blades of grass as he sang, "Nebber-snapper, flipper-dipper!"

He had started the song again when a loud, long creak made him stop and look up at the house. The front door swung eerily open and Bones's red kite danced in the doorway. Bones stopped and stared, utterly hypnotized by the sight of his very own kite, lost so long ago.

"Awesome kite," he murmured as he stumbled toward his treasured childhood toy. He reached out for the kite and, without realizing it, walked through the open doorway of the house. Then just as quickly as it had appeared, the kite disappeared, taking Bones along with it.

A moment later an awful, muffled scream came from inside the house. Then everything was quiet again.

CHAPTER 6

The danger zone was a huge construction site for a new condominium complex. DJ and Chowder called it the danger zone because their parents were constantly warning them about the site, saying that it was too dangerous for them to be around it.

DJ wriggled through the fence and stared at the huge foundation hole and the mammoth sections of shiny drainage pipe haphazardly placed in and around a maze of deep trenches. Above it all rose the tower of a six-story-tall crane.

Picking his way down the side of a trench, DJ called out softly, "Chowder?"

Suddenly Chowder sprang up in the cab of a backhoe parked near the base of the huge crane. Punching buttons, he made laser sounds, pretending to attack DJ.

DJ climbed into the cab. "Shut up! Nebbercracker is back from the dead," he informed his friend.

"No way!" retorted Chowder, his finger poised over the buttons on the backhoe control panel. Then he held up a key chain loaded with keys. "They leave the keys in here," he explained, gesturing at the control panel. Then, with a mischievous grin, he added, "You dare me?"

"You're not listening," DJ told him impatiently. "Nebbercracker is haunting me. His blood is on my hands, and now he's come back from the dead for revenge!"

Chowder shrugged and looked his friend over sympathetically. "You're really crazy right now, have you noticed that?" He juggled the backhoe keys in his hand. "I think," he offered, "you're just freaking out because you killed a guy today." He shrugged again before turning his attention back to the control panel and putting a key in the ignition.

"Life goes on," he said casually, "for you." Then he added, "Try to relax. Be cool. Like me."

Chowder leaned his elbow on the control panel to show how cool he was, and his elbow hit a green button. All of a sudden, with a loud rumble, the backhoe sprang to life, chugging and roaring. Chowder jumped out of his seat.

"Make it stop!" he yelled, all trace of coolness gone.

Calmly, DJ reached over and turned the key. The engine died and quiet returned.

"I need your help," DJ said.

Chowder smiled sheepishly. "Fine. You want my help?" he asked. "I've got three words for you . . . trick or treat."

"Fine. Let's go," DJ replied.

They left the construction site and walked along the empty streets of Mayville. The leafless trees lining the streets looked silver in the moonlight. Every once in a while a dog barked, or a lonely old tomcat let out a yowl, but otherwise the world was quiet and sleepy and peaceful as DJ and Chowder made their way to Mr. Nebbercracker's front lawn.

When they got there, the two boys hid behind a tree and peeked out. Before them, the Nebbercracker house seemed as unassuming as all the other houses on the block. But there was something else about it too, a watchfulness, a mysterious web of some weird consciousness that hung about the structure, dormant, yet ready to spring into instant awareness at any moment.

The proof of this was that the shades on the two upper windows had slowly risen as soon as DJ and

Chowder appeared on the sidewalk.

"Okay," Chowder said, withdrawing behind the tree when his staring intently at the house did not trigger a major response. "The haunting is subtle, yet really, really boring. Can I go home now?" He stood up to leave and DJ yanked him back down.

"Shh," DJ hissed urgently. "He'll hear you."

Chowder whispered back, "DJ, this is why nobody will sit next to us at lunch." Then he got an idea. "I'll go ding-dong ditch the house," he said brightly. "You'll see. No ghost."

Chowder then went into his commando act. He crawled out from behind the tree and slithered toward the house.

"Chowder, stop, please!" DJ pleaded. "Chowder, I'm serious!"

But Chowder ignored his friend. He found a bottle on the lawn and turned to tell DJ.

"Hey, DJ!" he called. "A bottle!"

"Chowder, put that down. Come back, please!" DJ called to him. Chowder put down the bottle and kept moving, crawling over to the porch steps.

Neither of them noticed as the grass around the bottle trembled and twisted and slithered toward it as if alive, enveloping it like tentacles and pulling it slowly down into the porous lawn—until not a trace of the bottle was left.

As the bottle vanished, Chowder walked up the steps. "Hey, DJ," he called from the porch. "Who am I?" Doing his best Nebbercracker impersonation, he yelled, "GET OFF MY LAWN!"

Chowder chuckled to himself, then rang the doorbell. Chimes sounded and suddenly transformed into a deep, vibrating growl that seemed to reverberate through the house. The two upstairs windows began to glow hideously with a blood red color. DJ's look of concern turned to horror as he yelled, "Run, Chowder!"

Too late! The door flew open and floorboards inside the house cracked and snapped into the doorjamb, forming a row of vicious-looking, chomping teeth.

Chowder screamed hysterically and leaped off the porch. Above him the shades on the red-glowing windows snapped open. Wood splintered and cracked as the windows contorted themselves to frown down at the boys, who started running away as fast as they could. At the same time, pipes burst, steam belched out, and the foyer of the house collapsed to reveal what looked like a pulsing red throat.

While frantically trying to get away, Chowder crashed into DJ and they both fell on the lawn.

They watched helplessly as the Persian carpet that covered the stairway slithered out of the house like a massive tongue and headed toward them. Rolling and dodging, the boys managed to avoid getting caught by the tongue as it snapped and whipped inches behind them. When the carpet retracted for a second, the boys took the chance to scramble away, the house following their retreat with its red-glowing window eyes and roaring loudly.

DJ and Chowder ran faster than they ever had in their lives, and the second they got into DJ's house, they slammed and locked the door behind them.

CHAPTER 7

When the doorbell rang the next morning, Zee was
sure it was Bones. She jumped up from the couch
and glanced at a mirror in the living room before
opening the front door. She had already started her
lecture. "Don't even think about crawling back here,"
she said, "'cause I'm—"

But it wasn't Bones at all. It was a little vampire.
Zee did a double take. It was twelve-year-old Jenny
Bennett, looking crisp and businesslike in her plaid
school uniform, except for the vampire mask.

"Boo!" Jenny said before taking off the mask and
sweetly chirping, "Trick or treat!"

Zee looked down at her, unimpressed, then closed
the door in her face.

The doorbell rang again. It was still Jenny,
completely unfazed. "Good morning, ma'am," she

said. "You've just witnessed a simulation of what you'll face this evening. Studies show that households that run out of candy are fifty-five percent more likely to be TP'ed."

Jenny gestured toward a wagon on the porch next to her. It was loaded with all sorts of candy. "To help avert this tragedy," Jenny continued, "I'm selling Halloween candy for my school, Westbrook Prep."

Zee nodded. "Good school," she said through a big yawn. "I got kicked out of there. Look, what do you want?"

"Just trying to get a head start on life and secure a successful future," Jenny responded.

"You want a successful future?" Zee asked. "When a guy with tattoos comes up to the drive-through, give him his burger," she advised, "not your phone number."

Jenny nodded. "Thanks for the advice. I'll be sure to make a note of it. But back to business." She took a breath and returned to her sales pitch. "Eggs, shaving cream, toilet paper. Without candy, I'm afraid your house is a bull's-eye with shingles."

"Nice try. This isn't my house," Zee informed her.

"Babysitter?"

"Yeah."

"Okay, let's cut the crap," said Jenny, with

renewed determination. "Maybe the parents you work for left you forty dollars in emergency money."

Zee shook her head. "Maybe they left me thirty."

"Maybe you give me twenty," suggested Jenny. "I write a receipt for thirty and you pocket ten."

"Maybe," Zee added, "and I want two extra bags of peanut clusters."

"One bag," countered Jenny, "and I'll toss in a licorice whip."

Zee held out her hand. "Deal." Then she added, with admiration in her voice, "You're good."

Meanwhile, DJ was up in his room with Chowder. The room was a mess, strewn with empty bottles of soda. The bed had been pulled across the room and stationed near the window. That made it easier to keep an eye on the monstrous house across the street.

It was Chowder's turn on the telescope. He covered his head with his Halloween cape as he stared at the house. At his desk, DJ was poring over data while clutching the key he'd found. He shuffled through Polaroids, examining them with a magnifying glass and a high-powered flashlight.

Chowder's watch beeped. Without glancing at it,

he said through his cape, "Eight a.m. No Detectable Movement."

DJ made the notation and went back to his Polaroids. Suddenly Zee burst into the room, "Hey, DJ! I got you some choco—"

The boys didn't bother to look up as they quickly shushed her and resumed their stakeout. Zee gave the room a once-over, grunted in disgust, and snapped the light on.

"No!" DJ yelled, throwing himself across the room to turn the light off. He toppled over a pile of plastic bottles. From the floor, he asked Chowder, "Any detectable movement?"

Chowder, already back under his cape, responded, "No Detectable Movement."

DJ gave a short sigh of relief before flashing an accusatory glare at Zee. The babysitter only shook her head and sighed in return. "What are you weirdos up to now?" she asked.

"Oh, nothing," retorted Chowder, throwing his cape back. "But something in the house across the street tried to eat us."

DJ got to his feet, scattering bottles in all directions. "We've been up all night watching it, haven't left this room once, not even to go to the bathroom."

"So don't drink that," Chowder threw in, pointing at a full bottle Zee was inspecting.

She made a face before tossing the bottle to the side and rolling her eyes. "You know, whatever disorder you guys have," she told them, speaking slowly, "I'm sure it has letters and I'm sure they have pills for it."

"Zee, I'm serious," DJ insisted. "There's something evil going on across the street."

Zee looked at him blankly for a moment and then rolled her eyes again. "Anyway, the reason I came up is," she said, "have either of you astronomers seen Bones? He left last night unexpectedly and never came back."

DJ and Chowder stared at her and then exchanged a worried look.

"Never came back?" Chowder asked. Zee shook her head.

"Bottle," said Chowder, remembering the bottle on Mr. Nebbercracker's lawn.

"Of course," confirmed DJ.

"Okay. You know what?" Zee said, completely exasperated. "I don't have time for this."

"Listen, Zee," Chowder said to her, putting a hand on her shoulder. "I don't know how to tell you this, but—"

"Your boyfriend has most likely been eaten alive," DJ interrupted.

With that comment, Zee felt it was time to leave. She tossed the bag of Halloween candy to DJ. "Breakfast," she explained, then left the boys alone in the darkened room again. The two glanced at the candy before looking grimly at each other.

Without a word, Chowder went back to the telescope. "Hello," he said suddenly.

"What? What is it?" DJ demanded, jumping up from his desk.

Not wanting DJ to see what he was looking at, Chowder quickly tried to cover. "Nothing," he lied.

But DJ didn't believe him. Lifting Chowder's cape, DJ crammed in next to him and muscled Chowder over, peering into the telescope with him.

It was Jenny. They both could see her then, and they jostled each other for a better view. As she sashayed purposefully down the street, her green school uniform gleamed in the soft autumn sun and her long red braids were a perfect complement to the russets and burnt umbers of the fallen leaves littering the sidewalk. Elbowing and shoving each other for control of the telescope, they got so distracted looking at Jenny's cute, businesslike little nose and big, bright, calculating eyes that they completely forgot about Mr. Nebbercracker and his mysterious house.

At least until the object of their admiration pulled her wagon up to the front walk of that house.

"Oh, no!" they shouted, racing out of the room and shoving past Zee on the stairs. "Hey!" she cried. "This isn't a playground!" just as the phone rang upstairs.

"That's your phone, DJ," she called after them. But they were already gone.

CHAPTER 8

"Hey! Hey! Yoo-hoo!" yelled DJ and Chowder as they exploded out of the house and hurried across the street. Jenny was already halfway up Mr. Nebbercracker's walkway when she heard them and turned around.

DJ stopped at the edge of the Nebbercracker lawn. "Don't go any farther," he told her, trying to be calm. "Come here."

"Yes," Chowder added as he nervously bounced from one foot to the other. "Over here!"

Jenny just stared at them for a moment and then flashed her best sympathetic smile.

"Are you guys mentally challenged?" she asked sweetly. "If you are, I'm certified to teach you baseball," she said.

As if right on cue, the window shades of the

house snapped up and the windows began to glow like hateful, glaring eyes. DJ and Chowder, still trying to appear casual, were unable to stop from looking up at them. Frowning, Jenny followed their gaze, spinning around like a majorette.

Then, with a loud wail from somewhere in the depths of the house, the front walk reared up, uncoiling like a huge snake and bouncing the unsuspecting Jenny into her wagon.

DJ and Chowder looked at each other and screamed, "Detectable movement!"

Then the front walk rose again and began to undulate. Jenny and her wagon were hurtled closer and closer to the house. Racing across the lawn, DJ and Chowder watched the door open and the mouth form as the wagon was pulled closer. Wooden teeth crashed together as the wagon hit the front porch. The boys, each one grabbing an arm, yanked Jenny out of the wagon just before the carpet tongue lashed out and scooped it up. The wagon was flung through the door, where it was promptly chomped into pieces.

Jenny and the boys fell in a tangled heap on the lawn before scrambling to their feet and running to safety across the street.

"Hey!" Zee's voice rang out.

Suddenly the walk ceased heaving, the front

door relaxed and closed itself, and the eyes became windows once again.

The kids turned to see Zee coming out of DJ's house. "There's an angry dad on the phone asking for the one called Chowder," she said.

Chowder jumped up to take the phone from her.

"He's worried about you," Zee added.

"He should be," snapped Chowder as he marched inside.

Zee walked across the street to confront DJ. "Start explaining," she demanded.

"The house is trying to eat us—," DJ began.

"Okay, stop explaining! I've had enough," Zee interrupted. Exasperated, she turned and started toward the Nebbercracker house.

"Where are you going?" DJ asked. Forgetting about Jenny, he ran after Zee and grabbed her arm.

Just when her shoe was about to touch the dreaded grass, she stopped. "What is your problem?" she asked.

Thinking fast, DJ said, "I'm going through changes!" He nodded his head, trying to look convincing. "Lots of changes!"

Zee mulled this over for a moment. Then she narrowed her eyes and looked at him closely. "No more Mountain Dew," she told him.

Nodding even more quickly, DJ agreed. "Right!"

Zee looked at him again and started to walk back toward the other side of the street. "I'm going to find Bones," she told him as she got into her car.

DJ nodded and smiled as widely as he could. "You have fun, okay?" he called out. "Don't worry, we'll be fine. And you tell him I said hi, okay? See ya!"

As she drove away, the smile drained from his face. Then he remembered that Jenny was still standing next to him.

"You wanna tell me what's going on?" she asked.

He looked at her. "I made the whole 'changes' thing up," he said, embarrassed.

Jenny looked at him blankly.

"I mean, didn't! Uh, I did, um . . . hi, I'm DJ," he said finally and shook her hand.

In DJ's room, Chowder paced back and forth, talking to his dad on the phone. It wasn't going well and he was just about to hang up. "Yes, Dad," he said. "I meant to call you, but—" He stopped talking for a moment and listened. "Yes, sir," he began again. "I know. Absolutely. Affirmative." He listened some more and then whispered, "I love you, bye," before pushing the end-call button.

Just then DJ ushered Jenny into the room. "And this is our little observation post, such as it were," he said, trying to seem cool. Glancing at the walls, he chuckled uncomfortably. "The posters are stupid," he told her. "I was gonna tear them down and put up some . . . art."

Seeing Jenny, Chowder put the phone back up to his ear. "Oh, yeah? Well, Dad," he said to the dial tone, "we'll see about that when I get home." He then hung up decisively on no one, put the phone down, and walked over to DJ and Jenny.

"Hey, DJ," he said, making his voice unnaturally deep, "you got any beer?" He then pretended to notice Jenny for the first time and smoothly added, "Well, hello there."

"This is Chowder," said DJ somewhat reluctantly.

"Charles to the ladies," Chowder corrected him, extending his hand.

Jenny took the hand in a businesslike grip and introduced herself. "Jenny Bennett," she told him. "Two-term class president at Westbrook Prep."

"Tough school to get into," said DJ.

"Yeah. I got in," put in Chowder casually, "but I decided not to go."

Jenny was not impressed. "It's a girl's school," she told him drily.

Chowder froze and stumbled. "Which is why I didn't—," he began, before deciding to change the subject. "You know, there's a great taco stand near there."

"I hate Mexican food," Jenny said.

"Me too," Chowder and DJ agreed unanimously. DJ gave Chowder a strange look and got one in return.

Jenny quickly tired of their banter and stepped over to the window. She stared at the now thoroughly normal-looking house across the street.

Chowder joined her at the window. "Fascinating, isn't it?" he said in his announcer voice, as if he were hosting a television show. "It just sits there, waiting. Mocking us with its"—he searched for the word—"houseness."

Jenny shot him a brief, pitying glance and turned to DJ. "May I please use your phone?" she asked.

Chowder held it out to her. She snatched it from his hand and dialed.

"Who are you calling?" DJ asked.

"Rude," Chowder scolded him.

"My mother," Jenny responded.

DJ sighed and shook his head. "She's probably not

going to believe you," he told her. "It's too much for the adult mind to comprehend."

Ignoring him, Jenny pointed at a full soda bottle. "Is this pee?" she asked. "Because if it is, that's really gross."

The boys tried to look as innocent as possible.

"DJ! You pee in bottles?" Chowder questioned, as if in shock.

"What are you talking about?" countered DJ "That's your pee!"

Chowder shook his head. "Nuh-uh. It's yours," he insisted.

DJ turned to Jenny. "It's his pee," he told her.

Jenny held her hand up, silencing them both. "May I please speak with Allison," she said into the phone. After a brief pause she added, "Her daughter. Thank you."

DJ whispered, "It's his pee."

Flashing her most polite smile, Jenny whispered back, "Excuse me," and left the room. As she walked into the hallway, they could hear her say, "Mom, I was selling chocolates in Mayville and a monster—," before she shut the door.

Alone together, DJ and Chowder stared at each other. DJ was the first to break the uncomfortable silence. "You hate Mexican food, huh?"

Nodding, Chowder said, "Uh-huh. You too?" They both knew they weren't really talking about Mexican food.

"Yeah," DJ confirmed. "In fact, you might say I started hating it first. Outside, in front of the house."

Chowder looked at him steely eyed, like a gunfighter in some Western movie. "Fine," he said. "Let's get technical. I started hating it through the telescope."

"You can't call dibs on a girl through a telescope," complained DJ.

"You can't call dibs on a girl," countered Chowder.

"Just did," DJ stated matter-of-factly.

"Me too," Chowder shot back.

They stared each other down until Jenny came back into the room, the phone in her hand. "She didn't believe me," she informed them.

Breaking off the staring contest, Chowder quickly changed focus and tried awkwardly to talk to Jenny. "Authority can be so . . . ," he began, rolling his eyes, making dumb noises, and twirling his finger by his head.

DJ, in the meantime, was hurriedly stuffing Bunny under his pillow.

"Okay," Jenny said, her glance shifting between

the two boys. "Normally I don't spend time with guys like you," she said. "But I just lost eighty dollars' worth of inventory, and I'm pretty sure that a house just tried to eat me. So you've got one hour."

She walked to the window and peered through the blinds. The boys joined her, and they watched as a mean-looking dog strolled onto Mr. Nebbercracker's lawn, sniffed around, and then squatted.

It was over in a second. The door flung open, the Persian carpet rolled out, and the dog was gone. Without even a chance to whimper.

Speechless, the three of them backed away from the window. Jenny finally broke the tense silence. "I think it's time to call the police," she said.

"Do you realize what's going to happen tonight?" DJ asked once they were outside and staring at the Nebbercracker house.

"Hundreds of kids," Chowder pronounced ominously, "coming right up that lawn . . . walking right up to that door."

"Trick or treat . . . only the trick's on them," added Jenny.

Suddenly the door to the old house opened and Chowder's basketball bounced out the door, coming to a rest at the bottom of the steps.

"Hey, my ball!" Chowder said, moving toward it.

"Chowder, no!" DJ said, holding him back.

The kids watched in horror as the house came alive again. This time, a board extended from the front porch and mysteriously transformed the basketball into the grinning face of a jack-o'-lantern. The house seemed intent on making mischief.

"It's going to be a bloodbath," said Chowder breathlessly.

Whheee-ooooo! A siren squawked, and a police car rolled to a stop beside the kids.

"Good news," Jenny said. "The cops are here."

CHAPTER 9

A fat, pink-cheeked cop named Landers rolled down the window and looked them over before speaking. "All right, kids, what's going on?" he asked. "I was in the forest wrestling with a bear claw when we got the call." Landers laughed at his own joke. "I was eating a donut!"

But before they could answer, the other cop, Lister, excitedly used the mike, his words blaring out of the loudspeaker like garbled static. "All three of you, step to the car now," the distorted voice ordered.

Landers rolled his eyes and hooked his thumb at his partner. "Rookie," he told the kids. "First week on the job."

Jenny approached the car in her most businesslike manner.

"Officer," she said to Landers, "we have reason to

believe that there is a dangerous creature inside that house."

"It may have killed a man," DJ added.

"And a dog," Chowder said.

Landers just smiled at them, but Lister sprang into action. Checking his belt, his gun, and his walkie-talkie, he said, "Doggie down. Oh, man. We got a situation!" Then he grabbed the police radio.

"What are you doing?" Landers snapped.

"I'm calling for backup," explained Lister. "You heard the kids! There's a dangerous creature inside that house!"

Landers gently pried the radio from Lister's hand and put it back on the dashboard. "There's no backup," he patiently told the rookie. "There's just Judy at the station. And this is no 'situation.'"

Lister looked disappointed.

"Just a couple of tater tots hopped up on too many pixie sticks," Landers explained.

Looking more dejected, Lister mumbled, "Why don't you ask the dog what he thought?"

"What was that?" Landers barked at Lister, who sulked quietly.

Landers turned back to the kids. "Time's up, peewees," he told them. "It's Halloween, and believe it or not, we got things to do."

He was about to drive off when DJ decided to give it one last try. "Wait, Officer! You've got to believe us," he pleaded. "It has a mouth that comes out and pulls things inside and eats them. Like this!" He made loud chomping sounds and motions with his mouth, stopping slowly as the cops stared at him.

Glaring in frustration at DJ, Jenny stepped forward. "The thing is," she began to calmly explain, "we're trying to make this sound more real than it normally would."

Landers looked at her. "The problem is," he said in a sarcastic tone, "it sounds . . . *not* real. So we'll see you later."

"No!" cried DJ. "All right. Watch this. I'll show you," he offered. "But if things gets out of hand—"

A thoroughly bored-looking Landers interrupted him. "We'll aim for Bigfoot," he said with a laugh, and then noticed Lister brandishing a gun.

"That's loaded!" Landers yelled, taking the pistol from his partner.

Trying to ignore the officers, DJ walked to the edge of Mr. Nebbercracker's lawn and carefully stepped on the grass. Nothing. He glanced back before taking a few steps toward the house. Chowder and Jenny held their breath.

But still nothing happened. Annoyed by the

loud laughter coming from the squad car, DJ tried a taunting dance, hopping around and stomping on the grass.

But there was No Detectable Movement.

"Smart house," commented Jenny drily.

Snatching up a rock, Chowder heaved it at the house, bouncing it off the weathered white siding.

Still, NDM.

The cops stopped laughing. "Hey, c'mere," Landers ordered them. DJ hurriedly walked off the lawn and joined Chowder and Jenny by the squad car.

Landers pointed at Chowder. "I'm gonna forget about that rock you threw." He jabbed his chubby finger at DJ. "Because that dance was pretty funny. But the next time I catch you messing with this guy's house, all three of you are going in the hole. Got it?"

No one replied, so he added, "You've got ten seconds to march."

"But we need your help," Jenny protested. "It's your job to help us."

Landers started counting. "One, two, three . . ."

Lister joined in on the loudspeaker. "Four, five, six . . ."

The kids looked at the cops one last time and then walked away. Following along in the squad car only inches behind them, Lister blared the siren—the final insult. The car butted up against Chowder, causing him to jump.

"Ow! That's tender!" Chowder cried.

"My house is right over there!" DJ protested.

"So much for relying on the government," Jenny said.

"Oh, man, we're screwed," Chowder said.

"No we're not," DJ said. "We'll go to an expert."

CHAPTER 10

The Pizza Freek was not exactly a place you'd expect to find an expert on anything. It was just a cheap pizza place with a few badly battered and scuffed plastic booths, a counter, and a cash register. The place was decorated for Halloween with some cardboard skeletons and witches that definitely looked like they'd seen better days.

At the end of a row of arcade games, at the far end of the Pizza Freek, an overweight, pasty, twenty-something guy feverishly worked the controls of a video game. He wore a stained Pizza Freek shirt, and an equally stained paper Pizza Freek hat covered his long-unwashed hair.

"You're looking at the three-time tristate over-fourteen Thou Art Dead champion," announced DJ, his voice full of awe.

On the wall hung a yellowed framed photograph of the same guy. In the picture he was much younger, though still just as pudgy and pale, with big circles under his eyes. He had on the same shirt he was now wearing, and a sash that read, "Knight of the First Order—1,000,000 Points!"

"His name is Reginald Skulinski. But they call him . . . Skull," DJ intoned.

Jenny didn't seem very impressed. "Who's 'they'?" she asked.

"Me and DJ," Chowder said. "He's the smartest guy on Earth."

"So let's go talk to him," suggested Jenny.

DJ and Chowder stopped her. "Skull is in the game zone right now. And you don't mess with him when he's in the game zone," warned Chowder.

"Well," Jenny said without hesitation, "if he's not coming out of the game zone, we're going in."

DJ and Chowder followed Jenny as she marched over to Skull, who was deeply engrossed in his latest game of Thou Art Dead.

"Did you see that?" he exclaimed, wagging a fleshy finger at the screen. "I just chopped off your head again! You can't even see it because your eyes are on your head!"

Reluctantly, Skull turned beady, red-veined eyes

There was no doubt about it. Something strange was going on in that house across the street. And DJ and Chowder were going to find out just what it was.

DJ and Chowder watched in horror as Jenny headed up the path to Mr. Nebbercracker's house.

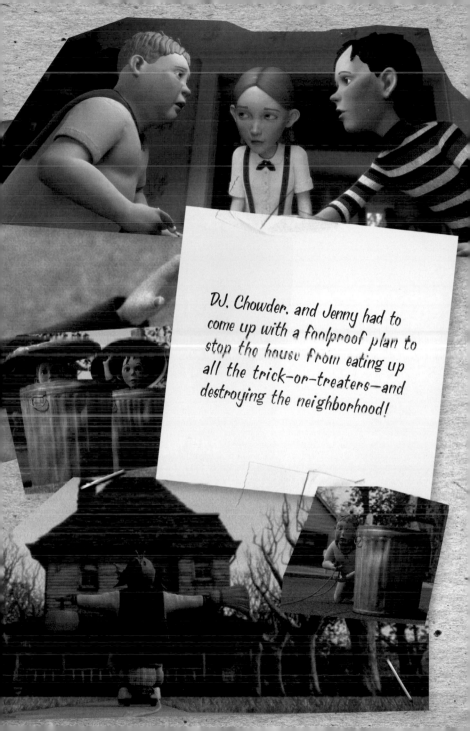

DJ, Chowder, and Jenny had to come up with a foolproof plan to stop the house from eating up all the trick-or-treaters—and destroying the neighborhood!

The house was ALIVE!

DJ and his friends had to figure their way out of the house.

CAN THEY STOP THE MONSTER HOUSE BEFORE IT'S TOO LATE?

on the three kids. "What? I'm busy playing a video game with my eyes not even looking at the screen. Spit it out."

DJ blurted out, "Old man Nebbercracker's house is possessed and I need to know how to destroy it before it comes out and tries to kill me—"

"Calm down!" responded Skull. "You make me want to throw up in some tinfoil and eat it!" he said before turning back to the game again. "Oh, you like the steel of my blade? It's so cold!" he whispered to the screen, finishing his move with a karate flourish.

"Possessed house, you say?" he said to the kids, hands flowing like liquid over the control buttons and joystick. "In my travels . . . to the video store and comic book conventions . . . I have seen many strange and wondrous things," he continued. "And I have heard tales of man-made structures becoming possessed by a human soul, so that the spirit becomes merged with wood and brick, creating a rare form of monster known as *Domus mactabilis.*"

"*Domus mactabilis.* That's Latin," Jenny informed the boys. "It means 'monster house.'"

"Oh, yeah," said Chowder, as if he'd known it all along. "That's Latin. One of my favorite languages. I love, love, love—"

"Look, kids," Skull scolded, "if you don't shut up, I'm going to eat all the hair on your head!"

His hands paused in their furious motion for a split second and then resumed. "For *Domus mactabilis* to come to be," he intoned, his voice deadly serious, "his home must be cherished by the man who lives there. And yea, he must perish in battle, defending his beloved home . . . from the murderous hands of his enemies."

His wisdom bestowed, Skull turned back to the video game and continued his virtual slaughter.

"So . . . how do we kill it?" DJ asked.

"All right, there is this one way, and it's simple," responded Skull. "You've got to strike at the source of life: the heart."

"But houses don't have hearts," said DJ.

"You might be right about that," Skull said. All of a sudden, the game captured his attention, and he furiously beat out a winning move. "It's gonna be fast, it's gonna be fast, watch this, whoo-hoo!" he yelled, hopping up onto the machine to finish off his opponent and then dancing around in victory.

"Did you see that, did you see that? That's like the hundredth time I've ever done that!"

As he danced, Skull's pager started beeping. He

picked it up and checked the message, then grabbed a pizza off the top of the game.

"Sorry, children, but I've got some very important business to take care of." Skull gave them a final once-over and bid them farewell. "I won't be seeing you later."

DJ, Chowder, and Jenny watched Skull slip out the front door to deliver another pizza—but not before he came running back to grab a quarter off the machine.

After their encounter with Skull, the kids headed back to Oak Street, mulling over what he'd said. They arrived in front of the Nebbercracker house and stood well back from the killer lawn.

"Okay," Jenny said. "So we need to strike at the heart."

"Yeah," Chowder agreed, "but where are we gonna find a heart inside a house?"

There was nothing to say. None of them knew the answer to that question. Examining the house, DJ wondered if Halloween was really doomed that year. How could this totally normal-looking house with normal-looking windows and doors and normal-looking smoke puffing out of the chimney in perfect, regular, little puffs be defeated?

Then he got an idea. "You know," he said, "ever

since Nebbercracker died, there's been smoke coming out of that chimney."

Chowder and Jenny looked up at the puffs of smoke appearing at a steady pace. Puff-puff, puff-puff—like a heartbeat.

CHAPTER 11

Back at home, DJ was putting finishing touches on a stakeout sketch of the Nebbercracker house when Jenny said, "We're gonna need to go inside."

Until then no one had said it out loud, but they all knew it was true.

"The furnace. We've only got two and a half hours till sundown," Jenny said. "We've got to figure out a way to get inside the house and put out the fire."

"Without being chewed to pieces," added Chowder matter-of-factly. DJ went over to see what Chowder had been doodling on the sketch pad. It looked like some kind of werewolf: big teeth, huge claws, glaring red eyes. Very scary.

Next to that were some stick figures. Chowder

was great at monsters, bad at people. They just looked like store dummies.

"Dummy!" DJ said, tapping the drawing.

"Hey, I was just doodling," Chowder said, taking offense.

"No, Chowder, this is it!" exclaimed DJ, pointing at Chowder's drawing. "First, we build a dummy," he said, the words spilling out in a rush. Snatching up Chowder's sketch pad, he quickly drew the monster house next to the stick figures. "We fill the dummy with a few gallons of cold medicine," he explained, glancing at Chowder. "You can borrow it from your dad's pharmacy."

"Say what?" protested Chowder.

But DJ barely heard him. "We feed the dummy to the house," he continued, drawing an arrow from one of the stick figures to the sketch of the Nebbercracker house.

"House eats medicine." DJ illustrated this by drawing Xs over each of the house's window eyes. "House goes to sleep. We get in, douse the fire, and get out," he finished, his voice triumphant, his eyes shining.

"Whoa, whoa, whoa, whoa," cautioned Chowder.

"Questions?" asked DJ.

Chowder thought for a moment. "Yes," he said

calmly. Then, unable to contain himself, he yelled out, "Are you nuts?" He turned to Jenny. She had to see how crazy this was. Making gestures and sounds to suggest that someone was losing his mind, he turned back to DJ.

"I don't want to steal drugs from my father," Chowder pleaded. "I don't want to go inside a monster. I don't want to die."

Looking as if he had made his case, he fell silent. Jenny looked from him to DJ, considered DJ's drawing for a moment, then spoke. "I say it's worth a shot," she said.

Hearing Jenny's response, Chowder immediately changed his stance. "I agree," he said. "Yes. Let's do it."

DJ smiled.

Chowder scooped up as many bottles of cough medicine in his father's closed pharmacy as he could and biked them back to DJ's house. While Jenny began constructing the outer layer of their dummy, DJ pulled out an old vacuum cleaner from the closet to use as its body.

Then they each grabbed a Super Soaker water gun from the toy chest.

Chowder eyed Jenny's extra-large Super Soaker. "Hey, uh . . . I wanted that one," he whined.

"You've got to be kidding me," Jenny said, rolling her eyes. But she exchanged water guns with Chowder anyway.

Now they were ready for battle.

CHAPTER 12

The setting sun had turned the rooftops of deserted Oak Street to a golden color as three large trash cans approached the Nebbercracker house.

In one of the trash cans was a trick-or-treater dummy shaped just like a vacuum cleaner. Chowder was pushing this trash can along, and when he got to the curb, he lifted the vacuum cleaner out—just as a strange groaning sound emanated from the house.

Chowder froze and glanced anxiously at the nearest trash can, carefully shifting the weight of the full Super Soaker slung over his shoulder.

Behind another trash can, DJ was ready with his own Super Soaker. He took one final look at the house before giving Chowder the signal to go ahead.

Chowder then placed the dummy on Mr. Nebbercracker's front walk. Then, keeping low and taking cover behind his trash can, he lined himself up with a third trash can, where Jenny was also armed with a Super Soaker. And she had a Wrist-Rocket slingshot that was locked and loaded.

Chowder smiled and gave her a thumbs-up. That was all she needed. Taking a careful, pinpoint bead on the house, she stretched the slingshot's elastic bands nearly to the breaking point. Her hands were trembling as she checked the target—and let fly.

Direct hit: doorbell!

Ding began the chimes, but the *dong* sounded more like a maddened wolverine, a crazed lion—a monster house. *DongGGGGGGRRRRRRR*. The window shades on the second floor flew open. The glowing windows tracked across the yard, their eerie gaze falling on the dummy.

"Trick or treat . . . ," Chowder called to the house.

"Plug it in," said DJ quietly.

Chowder put together the two extension cords he held in his hands. The roar of the vacuum cleaner shattered the strange quiet of the empty street as the dummy began to roll toward the front porch.

Right on schedule, the Nebbercracker front door opened wide. The house's teeth unsheathed and chomped viciously in expectation of what was to come.

It was working! DJ, Chowder, and Jenny smiled at one another.

Suddenly, *whheee-oooo!* The kids couldn't believe what they were hearing. It was the siren of the police cruiser . . . again.

The house's eyes slammed shut and its mouth vanished the instant the squad car turned the corner. The cruiser rolled over the extension cords and mashed a plug, stopping the dummy in its tracks. The kids buried their faces in their hands.

"So close," DJ said, sighing.

The same two police officers, Lister and Landers, pulled the patrol car up on the curb. Part of a tire touched Mr. Nebbercracker's lawn. Suddenly Lister burst out of the cruiser and leveled his flashlight on the kids.

Landers got out slowly and sauntered around to get a good look at DJ, Chowder, and Jenny. "Littering, loitering, vandalism, vagrancy," he recited, tsk-tsking as he took in the scene.

"And treason," added Lister excitedly.

"No, not treason," Landers corrected him patiently. Then he turned to the kids. "You kids come out from behind those trash cans," he ordered them.

"C'mon, you heard the big guy," commanded Lister. "Drop your weapons, pass them to me."

The kids did as they were told. Spotting the electrical cords, Landers followed them to the motionless vacuum cleaner. "I'm going to check this out," he informed Lister. "Stay here."

"I'm on it," Lister assured him, his flashlight trembling slightly.

Landers got to the dummy and was about to examine it when he felt someone at his side. It was Lister.

"What are you doing?" he demanded.

"I'm coming with you," responded Lister.

"I told you to stay there."

"I thought you were talking to the kids."

Landers's face turned deep red and he lost it. "No!" he yelled. "I was talking to you!"

Slinking back to the squad car, Lister grumbled under his breath, "You ain't gonna keep yelling at me like this. One of these days I'm gonna pop."

Forgetting about his partner, Landers resumed his investigation of the decoy. Tapping on the mask with his nightstick, he knocked it off and peered at the payload of cough medicine. He opened a bottle, dipped his finger in it, and put a little on his tongue. He spat out the liquid and glanced suspiciously at the kids. Then he turned around and took a long swig of the cold medicine before marching back to the car.

"That's it! That's it!" he announced. "We're taking them in."

Lister was thrilled. "That's what I'm talking about!" he said. "Where we taking them?"

"To jail!" responded Landers wearily.

"Right on! We get to use the jail!" exclaimed Lister, almost dancing for joy before he remembered he was supposed to be a serious cop. "Let's go," he told the kids sternly as he shoved them toward the car.

"You have to listen to us," DJ pleaded.

"Hey, two percent," said Lister. "You have the right to shut your mouth!"

He pushed DJ into the backseat. Jenny got in next. "The house is a monster!" she cried.

"And to think I believed you," Lister told her sadly as he turned to Chowder.

"Listen, I'm with you guys," Chowder said to the officer. "My cousin's a cop, in Milwaukee. I mean, kind of a cop. He has a gun. . . ."

Landers shot him a pitying look. "They're gonna love you downtown, Jughead," he said.

Once Chowder was in the car, Lister slammed the door shut and patted the top of the cruiser, feeling satisfied.

Then suddenly, from behind them, from

somewhere deep in the Nebbercracker house, a strange rumbling sound filled the air.

"You hear that?" asked Lister.

"Yeah. It's my stomach. I'm starving," replied Landers, wedging himself in behind the steering wheel. But Lister had other ideas.

"That sounds like the dangerous creature," he said, already halfway up the front walk of the house.

Landers rolled his eyes, annoyed. "This is like trying to wrangle a puppy," he said, sighing. To the kids, he said, "All right, I'll be back," then wiggled himself out of the car and followed Lister.

"No! No! Get away from there," screamed DJ as the three of them tried desperately to unlock the doors. But it was no use. Landers had locked the car doors from the outside, and the kids could not get out.

CHAPTER 13

DJ, Chowder, and Jenny watched as Lister zigzagged up toward the house like he was on some cop show, leaping onto the front porch, then slamming his body against the wall next to the door. Landers took a more leisurely approach, stomping reluctantly across the grass. When he came to the front porch, Lister pointed two fingers in the air with his thumb back.

"What?" queried Landers, not understanding the hand signal.

Lister went through the signal again more slowly and deliberately this time, but Landers still didn't get it. Frustrated, Lister put his finger to his lips, shushed Landers, and bolted off the porch, gun waving in the air.

But Landers stayed right where he was until the sound of glass breaking from somewhere in the house forced him, reluctantly and with much annoyed sighing, to investigate. As he stepped off the porch, he didn't notice the kids pounding on the windows of the squad car and screaming for him to get away from the house.

On the other side of the house, Lister noticed a strange swelling under the lawn. Taking his gun out, he pointed it at the ground and followed the swelling to where it ended at the base of a large willow tree near the porch. As he watched, the tree began to flex and move.

"Freeze, tree!" cried Lister, aiming his gun toward the willow. Suddenly the tree's branches snatched the gun from his hand. Petrified, Lister began to run, but the tree wound him up in its branches and hauled him into the air.

"What the—?" he screamed.

Hearing Lister's outcry, Landers raced around the house, took in the very spooky scene—and ran.

"Help!" Lister called out.

"I'm going for backup," Landers yelled back at him.

"You said there was no backup!" Lister shouted.

"I'm getting Judy!"

Making a break for the squad car, Landers almost got there, but the carpet tongue whipped out of the now open front door and dragged him inside—and the chomping wooden teeth closed on him! Right then and there, the willow tree gave a mighty swing, and Lister was hurled into the house as well.

Still locked in the squad car, the kids were huddled on the floor. They couldn't bring themselves to look. After a while they peered through the windows, only to see that the house was still, until . . .

SMASH! The car windows suddenly blew outward as something very heavy and not very friendly put a big dent in the roof, and the car was slowly lifted off the ground. It was the branches of the oak tree.

"Aaaaaahhhhhhh!" Chowder screamed.

The oak tree shook the car like a baby's rattle. And they were the rattlers!

"Mommy!" Chowder yelled as the three of them were bounced around inside the car. After what seemed like forever, the tree held the car over the middle of the lawn and the willow also bent forward, reaching out with its branches to hold part of the car. The car was now facing the house. Then, as if on cue, the front door began to widen, with a lot of loud creaking and cracking.

"This is all your fault," accused Chowder.

"What?" DJ asked, incredulous.

"I'm only here because of you!" screamed Chowder.

"Give me a break. You're here because of her," DJ protested as the car was drawn in closer to the widening mouth.

"*Same as you!*" Chowder yelled even louder.

Jenny, meanwhile, was staring through the front windshield at their approaching doom. "I don't believe this," she muttered to herself. Then she yelled out, "Will you both shut up! We're about to be killed!"

CHAPTER 14

Scrambling as far back as they could, the kids watched in horror as they were flung into the gaping mouth. The horrible wooden teeth eagerly clamped down on the car, slicing through its roof. DJ, Chowder, and Jenny screamed and clung to each other as the teeth became a wall right in front of their faces.

The siren gave up one last *wheee-oooo* as the teeth parted.

The tongue pulled the front half of the car down into its stomach, which was a broken beam and steel-lined pit in front of the quaking staircase. The kids watched as the tongue snaked out again and curled around the back half.

They could barely look as they were hauled toward the stomach with a massive jerk. At the edge, the tongue paused. They stared down into the monster's esophagus: a jagged tunnel straight down, lined with teeth.

The remains of the car lurched forward again. DJ decided it was time to do something. "Move!" he cried boldly, throwing himself through the shattered rear window and onto the trunk of the car. Jenny quickly followed him. They pulled Chowder out and rolled onto the floor of the house just before the carpet tongue tipped the back of the broken car into the throat. *Whoosh!* A strong gust of wind hit them as the house swallowed the rest of the car.

The kids ran for the front door, but the tongue was now moving toward it as well. Satisfied, the tongue seemed to lick its lips before resuming its place on the stairs. The walls, ceiling, and floor receded. The house returned to being a house, except that the floor rose and fell slowly. It was breathing. And from somewhere came a dull beating sound— *thump-thump*—like a heart.

DJ tried to grab at what was left of the door handle, but it quickly receded into the door.

"We're dead," moaned Chowder, flashing a look at DJ. "You killed us and now we're dead."

DJ raised his hand, motioning for silence. "I don't think the house knows we're in here," he whispered, turning on his flashlight. "It probably thinks we're still in the car."

Jenny turned on her flashlight. "Listen," she said quietly. "It sounds like it's sleeping."

Moving away from the door, DJ said, "The only way we're gonna get out of here alive is if we find the heart and put out the fire."

"Maybe we should examine our other options," suggested Chowder.

Shining his light on Chowder, DJ said, "Sure, other option: We wait here and do nothing until it wakes up and eats us."

"Find the heart and put out the fire. Got it," Chowder quickly agreed. He clicked on his flashlight and the three of them moved deeper into the house. They soon found a military cot and dresser, and there was also a pair of old World War II binoculars on a tripod. Gazing through the binoculars, DJ realized he was looking at his own house.

"He was watching me," murmured DJ to himself, surprised.

"DJ," Jenny called out, beckoning him to look at a picture she'd found. It was of Mr. Nebbercracker, standing proudly in uniform with some other soldiers. On it was written "The Demolition Squad."

Across the room, Chowder dropped a gas mask

he had found, making a loud clatter. DJ and Jenny immediately flashed their lights at him, shushing him.

"Sorry," Chowder apologized.

"Come on," said DJ. The three of them stepped farther into the foyer of the house.

"Be quiet!" Jenny whispered to Chowder.

"Don't worry, I have a very light step," he replied, before suddenly stopping. "There! Right there!"

Chowder was shining his light on something red and pulsing. DJ and Jenny focused their flashlights on it as well. They saw that it had once been a crystal chandelier. Now it was a damp, oozing tangle of wires dangling just in front of, and above, the throat.

Without warning, Chowder soaked it. Immediately the house shuddered and groaned, emitting a strange gagging sound as the throat yawned widely. Leaping to safety, the kids cowered against one wall as a light shone down from above, searching for the slightest movement.

"I thought if I shot the heart . . . ," whispered Chowder, paralyzed with fear.

"That's not the heart," Jenny whispered back. She pointed a trembling finger at the floorboards and the carpet. "Those are the teeth. That's the tongue . . . so that must be the uvula. It stimulates the gag reflex."

The house's shudders and creaks subsided and the relentless, searching light winked out.

Then the house seemed to quiet down and return to its strange regular rhythm. DJ tapped his foot gingerly on the floor. It felt solid again. Taking a deep breath, he tiptoed ahead, moving farther into the shadowy foyer.

"Okay, guys," he whispered to them when nothing happened. "Listen up. Let's move quickly and quietly. Don't touch anything."

He glanced around and took a step backward. "And stay togeth—"

There was a sharp crack and DJ let out a yelp before disappearing through the floor.

"DJ!" yelled Jenny. She and Chowder raced forward to where DJ had vanished. There was another loud snapping sound, and the floor gave way underneath them. Screaming in terror, they dropped into a dark void, freefalling through utter blackness and landing with a hard thud on what Chowder's flashlight revealed to be a huge mound of toys of all kinds piled together in the corner of a damp, long-neglected basement room.

"I'll save you," groaned Chowder when he caught his breath. Hearing a noise, he raised his Super Soaker and squirted wildly.

"Chowder! Knock it off!" Jenny whispered as the water hit her.

"Sorry, I thought you were a . . . ," Chowder began, swinging his flashlight around in a panic as he heard another noise. It was a wind-up toy monkey. As he trained his flashlight on it, the mechanical monkey abruptly stopped crashing its cymbals together, showed metal teeth at Chowder, and screamed three times. Chowder mumbled something and began to hyperventilate.

"Calm down," Jenny advised him. She shone her own flashlight on herself so he could see her and then asked, "Where's DJ?" When there was no answer, she called out again. "DJ!"

"Over here," came DJ's voice from a far corner. He was shining his own flashlight over something they couldn't quite make out.

"This must be where Nebbercracker kept his stash," Jenny said to Chowder as they waded through the toys that covered the floor and made their way to DJ.

"I think you should have a look at this," DJ said. The three of them held their breath as DJ passed the beam of his flashlight over metal bars and faded, ornately carved and painted wood. In the eerie silence, punctuated only by the dripping of water, the beating of their own hearts, and the rhythmic hissing of their own lungs, they realized they were looking at some kind of wagon. But not just any wagon. This was, unbelievably, a circus wagon. It must have been beautiful once, bright and beautiful and graceful.

Now, however, the wagon's vibrant colors were overgrown with mildew and mold and the whole thing was split down the middle as if smashed with a giant ax, the two halves held together by a rusty metal chain secured with a heart-shaped padlock. Across the wagon in large, fancy, old-fashioned letters were the words "Constance the Giantess."

"I've seen this before . . . ," DJ said, half to himself.

Chowder and Jenny looked at each other, speechless. DJ stepped forward to examine the padlock.

"The key," he said quietly as he pulled the key from his pocket. It matched the keyhole in the padlock exactly.

"Come on, DJ," urged Jenny. "We don't have time for this."

"Yeah," seconded Chowder, "we've got to find our way out of here."

Ignoring them, DJ slipped the key into the lock and stepped back. There was a series of eerie clicks that echoed strangely through the dark as it sprang open. The chain and lock fell to the floor. DJ grasped the bars of the doors, pulled them open, and went in. Chowder and Jenny, glancing nervously at each other, followed him.

Dust danced in the beams of their flashlights as the kids looked at peeling posters of Constance the Giantess. DJ shined his light at the floor and came across a slab of concrete. He traced the slab with his light—until he saw what looked like the shape of a molded human being.

"Constance!" DJ exclaimed.

"Holy moley," cried Chowder. "He really did eat her!"

"He couldn't have," said DJ. "Not when her whole body is buried in cement."

"Look at all this stuff," said Jenny, inspecting all the memorabilia scattered around the caravan. "Why would he build her a shrine if he had murdered her?"

"Maybe he just felt guilty or something," said Chowder. "Can we get out of here?"

DJ moved closer to the face of the concrete slab. "I always knew you were hiding something, Mr. Nebbercracker," he murmured.

Just then the floor began to shake and DJ tripped. The ripple effect of the quake caused the concrete slab to crack and break apart—revealing a human skeleton!

Rubbing their eyes in disbelief, the kids looked around them as pipes flailed and boards cracked and a scream was heard. Somehow, the mold, dust, and grime of the house, along with the boards and wires, had all coalesced into a vague, menacing portrait of the huge woman they had just seen buried in the cement.

"It's her!" shouted DJ over the desperate rumbling scream of the house.

Jenny looked at him in wide-eyed shock. "She attacks anyone who touches her," she said in a surprising monotone. "Even one tiny little bit."

"And we're trapped inside," added Chowder.

The three of them exchanged glances as the basement exploded into throbbing, violent life. All around them the house shook and tossed about on its foundations, the very bricks and mortar of the place uprooting themselves from the ground in explosions of dirt and dust and debris. Joists cracked and broke into pieces. Pipes split and greasy, foul-smelling water sprayed into the air as the house shivered and buckled. The destruction was accompanied by a roaring sound and the crackle of electricity arcing like lightning as power lines foul-smelling water sprayed into the air as the house shivered and buckled. The destruction was accompanied by a roaring sound and the crackle of electricity arcing like lightning as power lines snapped and writhed like snakes, emitting showers of sparks and illuminating the basement in bursts of glaring white light.

Constance had noticed them at last.

CHAPTER 15

The evil house woke up, heaving and growling as pipes exploded and the walls and the floors convulsed all around them.

"Run!" yelled DJ.

The searchlight glare from the window eyes turned inward and sought them out. The throat opened hungrily and the searchlights shone into the basement, spotting them.

"Hide!" Jenny shouted.

The kids screamed and ran in three different directions.

Chowder, diving behind a pile of toys, spotted his basketball, bouncing through a section of the house.

"My ball! Come back!" he said, chasing after it.

"It's a trap!" yelled DJ as he braced himself against a wall.

At that moment huge springs exploded out of the ceiling like giant Slinkys, snatched Chowder in their coils, creaked menacingly, and hauled him upward. Chowder screamed as he bounced through the moldy old plaster ceiling and careened past beams studded with rusty nails, nearly suffocating in smelly blankets before finally coming to an abrupt halt.

For a moment everything was perfectly still. What had happened? Where was he?

Chowder tried to move his legs and realized that from the waist down he was stuck in the ancient iron springs of an oversize bed, which was covered with a lacy, foul-smelling red bedspread. As he gazed around the room, struggling for breath, he saw mold-covered stuffed animals and ragged, frilly curtains covering dirty, streaked windows. In an instant he knew where he was, and he knew whose room he was in.

It was Constance's.

Hearing a creaking, hissing sound from behind him, Chowder twisted around to see more bedsprings rising around him like cobras. They creaked and squealed, the tortured old metal coils shedding rust and grime in a cloud of orange-gray dust. Chowder knew he had to get free before the animated springs decided to attack. Working furiously, he managed to get an arm loose. Then, freeing his other arm, he fought off the living springs, punching and kicking at them as he struggled out of their rasping, metallic clutches. Jumping off the bed, he untangled himself from the bedspread, aimed a last kick at the straining, demonic springs, and ran out the bedroom door.

At the same time, Jenny had been swallowed up by living pipes, which slithered and writhed around her. They dragged her, struggling, into the kitchen. But Jenny would not go without putting up a fight. Dispatching the pipes with a few well-placed kicks and the help of an old cast-iron skillet, which she swung like a major league slugger, she got away from them and ran gasping into the foyer, which was now tilted at an impossible angle.

Seeing DJ scrambling to hold on as the house continued to tremble and quake and roar, Jenny raced over to him. At the same time, Chowder appeared at the top of the stairs. He looked like he was about to shout something, but the house was one step ahead of him.

DJ and Jenny watched helplessly, then closed

their eyes as the stairs collapsed and Chowder slid toward the throat, dug his nails into the banister, and held on. It was no use. The old wood was too soft. It cracked and gave way under his weight. Flailing helplessly, Chowder slipped and slid toward the house's hungry throat as the house itself let out a terrifying, victorious roar. Chowder screamed as he went over the edge and then screamed even louder as he managed to grab one of the broken, jagged floorboards that ringed the house's stomach.

When DJ and Jenny dared to look again, they saw Chowder holding on for dear life as the house bucked and quaked in an attempt to shake him off. DJ had to act fast to save his friend. Carefully stepping around the edge of the black pit, he wedged himself—securely, he hoped—into the debris left by the collapsed stairway. Then he reached down—and almost fell into the pit himself.

Despite the house's contortions, DJ finally found Chowder's wrist and, grunting and heaving, slowly hauled him to safety.

"DJ, look out!" screamed Jenny.

The carpet tongue was coiled up like a cobra behind DJ, ready to strike. Without warning, it lunged, darted in, and hungrily snatched DJ. Chowder was left to struggle for himself, half in and half out of the pit, as DJ was raised high in the air, shaken back and forth, and then dropped unceremoniously into the pit.

"Noooooo!" cried Jenny. Desperate for an end to the chaos, she suddenly remembered the uvula. She climbed and forced her way up the flattened stairs before taking a deep breath and doing a swan dive off what was left of the banister, flinging herself into the air, and catching the uvula.

With Jenny hanging on to its tip, the uvula stretched, causing the house to buck even more violently. Suddenly she was thrown off. Flying through the air, her eyes clenched shut, she caught hold of something and held on. When she opened her eyes, she realized that it was DJ—she had been thrown onto DJ, who was miraculously clinging to Chowder's stubby legs. Momentarily relieved, she looked up to see the uvula shooting back to its place in the ceiling. It crashed into the plaster and rained debris down the throat, and in an instant, everything stopped moving.

The tongue lay down. A few pipes burst. There was a loud, convulsive heaving sound from deep in the house. The three children sensed that something major was about to happen—but what? Then the house retched and the door opened. All three children were hurled out onto the sidewalk amidst tons of water and debris.

"Did we just get upchucked?" asked Chowder a few moments later, slightly dazed.

"The uvula. Nature's emergency exit," Jenny said.

The kids heard the house groan again, which made DJ jump up and run into the street—just as a car screeched around the corner and headed toward him!

CHAPTER 16

With brakes squealing, the car lurched to a halt only
inches from DJ. It was a taxi. The door opened and
an ominous figure emerged, hunched and deathly
pale.

It was Mr. Nebbercracker—in a hospital gown!

"A ghost!" wailed Chowder, grabbing Jenny and
using her like a shield. "Begone! Fie!" he spat at the
old man.

Mr. Nebbercracker shoved past the stunned DJ.
"Begone yourself," he retorted angrily. "Get away!"

"He's not a ghost," said DJ. "He's not dead. I'm
not a murderer!"

"Of course I'm not dead. Who said I was dead?"
complained Mr. Nebbercracker. "You'll be dead if you
don't scram! Don't you know what day this is?"

The kids just stood there watching as Mr.

Nebbercracker turned toward his house.

"Honey, I'm home," he said to the house, and it began to sob and cry piteously.

"Look at you. Your shingles are ruffled. Your windows are cracked," the old man told her in a soft, comforting voice. "But it's no problem, sweetheart. It's no problem at all. Nothing a little paint and varnish can't handle."

The house groaned, agitated.

"Let's not do anything foolish!" continued Mr. Nebbercracker, soothing the house. "What do you say I come in, we'll turn those lights down, and we'll spend a nice quiet evening. Like we do every year. No kids, no distractions. Just us."

"It's her," DJ said, amazed. "The house is her." He began to walk toward it.

Chowder and Jenny pleaded with DJ to come back, but DJ called out to Mr. Nebbercracker.

"Mr. Nebbercracker," he said. "I know about Constance."

The house rumbled in surprise as Mr. Nebbercracker turned to DJ.

"What?" Mr. Nebbercracker demanded. "What do you know? You don't know anything!"

The house rumbled ominously, as if in agreement.

But DJ held his ground. "I saw her," he said.

"You were in my house?" Mr. Nebbercracker cried out as he staggered back in dismay. DJ reached out and steadied the old man.

The house grumbled again, this time more loudly.

"You didn't kill her, did you?" DJ said gently.

"I love her so much," Mr. Nebbercracker said. Seeming to recognize DJ for the first time, the whole story came pouring out of him in such a heartfelt, eloquent way that the kids looked around in wonder as they imagined themselves peering through the bars of the circus caravan at a crowded circus midway. Hurdy-gurdy music filled their ears, and the smell of popcorn and cotton candy permeated the bright, sunshine-filled early morning air.

Outside the wagon, people in old-fashioned clothes pointed and laughed at them, throwing half-eaten ice creams and candy wrappers through the bars at the caravan's sole, unhappy inhabitant.

Constance.

Grotesquely obese but beautiful in her own way, the woman heaved a labored sigh and endured the mockery of the crowd with a downcast, resigned expression on her heavily made-up face. Mr. Nebbercracker told them how he had first seen her.

It had started with a young boy in knickers and a newsboy cap. The boy approached the bars of

Constance's caravan and smiled sweetly at the huge woman. For the first time, Constance smiled too, only to be hit with a tomato a second later—thrown cruelly at her by the same boy. It hit so hard that the tomato splatted loudly against her chest.

Constance's smile disappeared and was replaced with a look of hurt, which morphed quickly into anger. Pulling her great bulk out of her chair, Constance cursed and roared at the boy. But the boy only laughed and was about to launch another attack when a man grabbed his arm and took the tomato out of his grimy hand. He was a young man in a smart khaki uniform.

Mr. Nebbercracker!

Mr. Nebbercracker—Horace—told them how he'd comforted Constance in her caravan that night after the crowds had gone.

"There, there, dear. It'll be all right," he had assured her, gently wiping the tomato from her dress.

She smiled at him. It was a small, tentative smile showing that, for perhaps the first time in her life, Constance was beginning to trust someone.

Mr. Nebbercracker recalled how he had hitched her caravan to a truck and hauled his beloved Constance away from the circus, and how they danced for joy as they chose and settled on the site of the future Nebbercracker house.

"We're home, my dear," Horace Nebbercracker had told his bride, and they danced some more. Then Mr. Nebbercracker related how he had cleared the land, chopped down the trees, and begun to build the house.

"And one day," Mr. Nebbercracker told the kids, "I decided to do away with that awful cage my poor Constance had endured for so long."

In the now distant past, Mr. Nebbercracker raised an ax and smashed it down, the blow accompanied by a bloodcurdling scream.

Was he killing Constance?

No. Mr. Nebbercracker was intent on destroying the painful memories attached to Constance's circus caravan by destroying the caravan itself. He had chopped Constance's caravan nearly in half as he waited for the cement mixer to prepare the concrete for the basement foundation of the house that he and Constance were to share.

At that moment Constance ran into view, nearly hysterical.

"Are you hurt?" he asked her, setting down the ax.

"Yes," she cried, pointing a giant finger at two Halloween-costumed boys with eggs in their hands. "Those criminals are assaulting my house."

"They're just a couple of kids, dear," he assured her. "It's Halloween."

"No! It's my house and they're hurting it," she screamed.

As a couple of eggs splattered on the ground near their feet, Horace tried to reassure her. "Calm down, my dear." To the boys, he shouted, "Go on. Scat!"

"They'll never stop," Constance cried.

"Constance, listen to me," Horace Nebbercracker told her. "As long as I'm here I won't let anything bad happen to you."

That trusting hint of a smile appeared on her lips, the same as in the caravan so many years before—just as a barrage of eggs flew past her.

Filled with fury, Constance shouted, "You hooligans! You vandals! You think you can attack without any consequence? You think I won't defend myself? I'll teach you a lesson!"

But the eggs kept coming, and one even landed on her chest. Constance screamed as she slipped in the gooey mess. Flailing at Mr. Nebbercracker for help, she accidentally knocked him to the ground with one mighty, hamlike fist. As he fell, Constance lost her own balance and went teetering backward, closer and closer to the newly dug foundation. Reaching out a massive arm, she clutched at the cement mixer.

The cement mixer broke her fall, but her weight proved too much for the machine, and slowly, inch by inch, the lever began to tilt. And Constance screamed one last time as she fell into the pit that would be her grave. The cement, the intended foundation of her future home, poured in on top of her, entombing her completely within minutes. Her scream echoed in the ears of the kids as Mr. Nebbercracker's story ended and they found themselves once more in the street.

"So I finished the house," Mr. Nebbercracker said to DJ. "She would've wanted that."

DJ nodded, deeply saddened by his neighbor's tragedy.

"She died, but she didn't leave," Mr. Nebbercracker continued. "I had to keep her under control. And on that one night every year . . . I had to take precautions."

DJ remembered Mr. Nebbercracker's KEEP OUT! and BEWARE! signs, but kids threw eggs on Halloween anyway, even as Mr. Nebbercracker screamed at them to get away.

"We're still together," explained Mr. Nebbercracker. "I take good care of her."

He turned around to address the house. "I take good care of you, don't I, honey?" he asked. "When your floors bow, I hammer them down! And I shine it, and I keep the lawn clean and fresh. . . ."

Mr. Nebbercracker turned back to DJ. "And I keep you kids off of it! I have to! She attacks anyone who comes near!"

The house rumbled dangerously again.

"Coming, dear," Mr. Nebbercracker responded hastily. Then he yelled to DJ, "Go!"

But DJ grabbed his arm. "No, wait! I can't let you do this, Mr. Nebbercracker," he said. "I know you've been protecting us kids all these years." He paused before adding, "And I know what it's like to have everybody in the neighborhood think you're a weirdo."

"Do you?" asked Mr. Nebbercracker.

"Mr. Nebbercracker, you don't have to live like that anymore," DJ told him. "Let her go."

The house growled fiercely.

"But if I let her go," the old man responded sadly, "I'll have nobody."

DJ shook his head. "That's not true," he said, "you'll have me."

He held out his hand—and his elderly neighbor took it. Filled with more hope than he had felt in a very long time, Mr. Nebbercracker allowed DJ to lead him away.

But the house was not so forgiving. With an earsplitting shriek, the house groaned and shook. Then, incredibly, it pulled itself out of the ground.

The uprooted basement of the house split down the middle, and it took its first step, right out of its foundation. Pulling the nearby trees in close to use as arms, the house took another step and emerged fully from its hole in the ground. Then it emitted a triumphant roar.

DJ and Mr. Nebbercracker wasted no time. They ran. Shaking the ground as it moved, the house stomped after them. It cast a monstrous shadow over the entire block. It flattened cars and uprooted trees, getting steadier with each earth-shattering step.

The house got caught in some electrical lines and tore the poles from the ground, sending them crashing and sizzling down all around. It was gaining speed—and Mr. Nebbercracker was slowing down.

Rounding a corner, the kids raced ahead. Without even thinking about it, they were headed for the danger zone—the condominium construction site.

As they hopped a fence, DJ glanced back to see Mr. Nebbercracker struggling. "I'll be all right," he called weakly. "Go on!"

DJ ran back to prop the old man against a Dumpster, hoping he would be safe there. Chowder called out to DJ, "Run!" There was a thundering crash behind them, and another. The house rose above the horizon and flattened a stone wall just as the sun began to set. Glancing one last time at Mr. Nebbercracker, DJ and Chowder took off. They caught up with Jenny and ran into the danger zone.

The house thundered up to the fence and paused. It seemed to be looking for something—Mr. Nebbercracker, presumably. Then it stopped. The second story craned forward, its window eyes shining.

Just then a brick sailed through the air and glanced off the house's roof. The house cried out in pain and turned to find its attacker.

It was Mr. Nebbercracker himself, with another brick ready. "You stay away from those children, Constance," he cried.

But Constance ignored his plea. Charging angrily, the house towered over the old man, ready to strike. Then suddenly, at the last moment, Constance seemed to recognize the man who had once been her husband. The house clacked its front door shut and looked at him calmly.

"There, there, Constance," soothed Mr. Nebbercracker as the house settled down, the clang of pipes and the creak of wood coming from somewhere deep inside. "You've been a bad girl, haven't you? You've hurt people. Well, we've always known this day will come. I've got to make things right."

As he said this, Mr. Nebbercracker carefully pulled a bundle of dynamite from his sling. Moving slowly, he lit the fuse. Sensing the dynamite, then seeing the flame, the house reared up, howling in rage and terror.

"Constance! I've always done what's best for you, haven't I?" Mr. Nebbercracker said sternly.

The door flew open and the hardwood teeth started their chomping motion. The tree arms started reaching down to strike at Mr. Nebbercracker, when suddenly a bright light appeared and a thunderous roar rang out.

It was the massive backhoe—with Chowder, DJ, and Jenny at the controls!

Gunning the engine, they smashed through the fence and charged at Constance.

"Leave him alone," they yelled at the house.

"Yeah! Get your grubby branches off the old man," added Chowder as he punched wildly at the buttons on the control panel.

"Chowder, how do you know how to drive this thing?" Jenny asked, terrified.

"I don't," Chowder replied as he pulled a lever.

CHAPTER 17

Chowder hit a button that sent the backhoe arm crashing into the side of the house. "Take that!" he yelled.

The house roared, lashing out wildly and hitting Mr. Nebbercracker, who flew into the air.

"Oh, no!" cried DJ, grabbing a walkie-talkie. He leaped from the machine and rushed over to Mr. Nebbercracker, who lay helplessly behind some bushes.

"Here, take this," the man croaked. "Help me finish what I started." Mr. Nebbercracker held the still-lit dynamite out to DJ. "We've only got a few minutes."

"How many?" DJ asked.

"Three minutes, eighteen seconds!" Mr. Nebbercracker yelled, then a beat later, "Three minutes, fourteen seconds!"

DJ hesitated for just a second and then took the dynamite. He carefully studied the house, looking for a target. The door was shut. Then he saw the chimney.

But before he could do anything—*STOMP!*

With a massive step, the house knocked DJ off his feet and sent Jenny flying out of the backhoe. She tumbled down the steep slope into a ditch. Moments later DJ nearly landed on top of her. Jenny's eyes went wide when she saw the lit dynamite.

"DJ, get rid of that!" she exclaimed.

"I'm working on it," he told her.

Picking himself up, DJ saw the backhoe and the house battling at the top of the embankment. One minute Chowder was pushing forward, and the next the house was pushing him back, nearly sending the machine down the slope on top of them. Scanning the danger zone, DJ focused on the towering crane and got an idea.

"Chowder! I need you to get the house down under this crane," he said into the walkie-talkie. "Think you can do that?" he added. Then he grabbed Jenny's hand and pulled her toward the crane. DJ pointed up at the crane. "Climb!" he ordered.

Jenny looked doubtful.

"C'mon! For Chowder," DJ urged her.

DJ's walkie-talkie crackled, and Chowder's voice came in loud and clear. "Piece of cake."

In the backhoe, Chowder jammed a heavy lever and threw the massive machine into reverse. He caught the house off guard, and it struggled mightily against the earthmoving machine. But the battle between the backhoe and the house caused both to lose their balance, and they plunged down the embankment in a huge cloud of dust and debris.

Chowder screamed as he was tossed about in the cab. The backhoe hit the ground with a heavy thud as the monster house plummeted down the slope and seemed to explode. Walls flew off, shingles and planks peeled away, pipes dangled, floorboards splintered. The house smashed into a million pieces.

DJ and Jenny had climbed halfway up the crane when they saw the house go down. They nearly started cheering when they realized something awful: Where was Chowder?

Then a familiar voice came crackling over the walkie-talkie. "Hey, guys," Chowder said. "Look who just won—it's me, the screwup!"

But they had no time to congratulate one

another. Horrible cracking, grating, grinding, and smashing sounds could be heard over the gentle whistling of the autumn night wind. At first there was still so much dust in the air that it was hard to tell what was happening, but as the dust began to clear, and the grinding and cracking and groaning became louder, the kids realized that their worst fear was coming true.

The scraps of the house shook and shuddered. A loud roar cut through the cool air as shingles whirred through the dark like axes, bricks smashed into each other like shots from a cannon, and shards of glass leaped up from the ground and stitched themselves together into cracked, monstrous windows. The house had reassembled itself into an even more nasty, jagged, and ugly monster!

"Wait! You can't do that! It's not fair!" cried Chowder.

The gnarly new beast house charged the backhoe. Chowder slammed the machine into gear and hit the gas, heading for the crane.

DJ and Jenny climbed the rest of the way to the top of the crane and into the operator's cabin. From there, they watched the scrap heap of a monster house get closer and closer as it chased Chowder.

"Chowder! Keep it coming!" DJ said into the walkie-talkie, glancing at his stick of dynamite. The fuse was definitely shorter.

Chowder poured on the gas. The backhoe rumbled toward the crane. The house's chimney was just about level with DJ.

Chowder blasted the horn. "You ain't nothing," he taunted the monster. "You're a shack! An outhouse!"

The house charged forward with a deafening roar. Chowder frantically pounded all the buttons and made the claw of the backhoe smash its face, which made the ugly house even madder.

Stretching its mouth wide open, the house clamped down on the claw and lifted the backhoe off the ground. It swung the machine in the air and Chowder was thrown from the cab like a rag doll, landing with a solid thump on the ground—just as the monster house devoured the backhoe whole.

But it was not satisfied. The house now turned its attention to Chowder and stomped after him. From the top of the crane, DJ and Jenny now had only one thought: Chowder was going to die!

"Hold on, Chowder! I'm coming," yelled DJ. He had to get out to the end of the enormous crane arm and release the hook. If he could do that, he could swing on the cable and get a good shot at the house with the dynamite. But he was a hundred feet off the ground.

"I can't," DJ cried, terrified.

"Yes, you can," Jenny encouraged him. When he still made no move to leave the operator's cabin, she kissed him. "You can," Jenny told him again. "For Chowder."

Surprised, DJ smiled and looked at the crane arm with renewed confidence. Jenny was right. He could do it. He had to—for Chowder.

DJ handed the dynamite to Jenny, who glanced nervously at the now dangerously short fuse. "When I say 'now,' in a minute, throw this to me," he told her, stepping carefully out of the cabin, wind whistling in his ears, and onto the crane arm.

Far below, Chowder was about to be eaten. The house snapped and raged at him while he dodged and rolled just in time, but how long could he keep it up?

Hand over hand, DJ climbed the crane arm. "It's not as bad as it looks," he repeated over and over again. Inching forward, DJ forced himself out and up the crane. After what seemed like hours, he was standing at the very end of the crane arm. Hanging above him was the cable and at the end of that, suspended in empty space, the large metal hook with which he hoped to save Chowder's life. Hoisting himself up, he wedged a foot into the hook and reached up with his other hand toward the cable release that would send the hook—and him with it—flying through the air to Chowder's rescue.

"Please let this work," DJ pleaded to himself as he fumbled with the release mechanism. Hearing a snap, his eyes went wide as the hook and the cable release gave way.

"Now!" DJ yelled, holding his arm out for the dynamite as he sailed past the operator's cabin in a great sweeping arc.

Jenny took aim and tossed him the dynamite just as the monster house snapped Chowder's cape up in its gnashing, wooden jaws and hoisted him into the air.

The dynamite landed right in DJ's outstretched hand. He smiled with relief at Jenny and then grimaced at what was left of the sputtering, sparking fuse—almost nothing! He had to throw it.

Swinging toward the house, DJ could see the chimney directly ahead of him. He had only one chance to get it right.

Closer and closer he swung. Then he was looking

right down into the glowing, pulsing heart of the beast.

He let the dynamite go. And it was a direct hit!

As the dynamite went down the chimney, the house seemed to freeze. Chowder saw his chance to escape. He untied the cape around his neck and tumbled into the dirt, then scrambled away as fast as he could.

The house settled with a groan. In that moment, with the moonlight shining down on it, it looked almost peaceful. It seemed somehow to have found a way to change itself back into the well-cared-for and innocent white clapboard house it had once been.

But the kids knew it wasn't over just yet. Waiting breathlessly for the house's next move, the kids heard a kind of low rumbling. They braced themselves for some new onslaught from the unstoppable house, certain that they had failed. Not even dynamite could pacify the restless spirit of Constance. As the rumbling grew louder, they got ready to run.

Then the house exploded.

In a huge, booming fireball, the walls blew out in four different directions. Wood, glass, and metal, bricks and concrete shot up into the air. The mushroom cloud of debris sent the burning roof rocketing spectacularly upward into the night sky like a shooting star.

The kids were wide-eyed with disbelief as they followed the roof's trajectory into the sky. When the burning remains thumped back into the dirt, they turned from its glowing embers, looked at one another, and began to cheer. They'd done it! Constance was finished! Jumping for joy and shouting out loud, they hooted and high-fived until their voices and hands were raw. Finally, when they were so out of breath that they couldn't do one more "Hoo-yah!" they heard the sound of someone crying. It was Mr. Nebbercracker, standing with his face in his hands.

Just then a sort of whooshing sound from the direction of the remains of the house made them turn. The cloud of dust raised by the destruction of the possessed house began to swirl curiously in the still air. As they watched, the dust rose, glowing with a strange, soft light of its own.

Huddling together as the strange cloud billowed above them, the kids watched, fascinated by how quickly the mass of mysterious dust was swirling and picking up speed. It fanned out, as if searching for something. Pausing above the weeping figure of Mr. Nebbercracker, the cloud of dust slowly stopped moving and transformed into the vague, transparent, radiant form of his long-ago love.

"Constance," the kids said with a gasp.

Looking up, Mr. Nebbercracker recognized his beloved in the swirling dust and cried loudly. "My dear . . . , good-bye," he sobbed.

At that, the apparition of the doomed Constance smiled gently. An arm formed out of the dust that sparkled in the evening light. Whirling down, it folded around Mr. Nebbercracker in a final, loving embrace. Overjoyed to feel Constance's touch once again, Mr. Nebbercracker looked lovingly at the vision of his former wife. The swirling shape of Constance wavered, then vanished, reappeared, and, with a soft sigh, disappeared once again—this time forever. The fine debris out of which the magical cloud had formed cascaded to the ground with a dry, tinkling patter.

"Wow," muttered Chowder as he and DJ and Jenny exchanged a look of wonder at what they had just witnessed.

Mr. Nebbercracker was still crying. Trying to make him feel better, DJ shrugged at Chowder and Jenny and approached his neighbor. "I'm sorry about your . . . house, uh, wife," he said. "I mean your house-wife."

"Trapped for forty-five years," cried the old man. "And now . . ." He looked at DJ before grabbing him and hugging him tightly. "We're free! Thank you, friend," he gushed. Looking at Chowder and Jenny, he smiled gratefully at them through his tears. "Thank you all."

CHAPTER 18

That Halloween night Mayville was packed with trick-or-treaters. There were ghosts, goblins, fairy princesses, witches, and monster killers.

At the end of Mr. Nebbercracker's ruined front walk, Jenny and DJ stood handing out toys to all the costumed children. They would call down to Chowder, who was standing in the hole where the basement used to be. Chowder then tossed up a toy from the pile the house had once taken: a Frisbee, a baseball, a model airplane, a toy train. . . .

"Happy Halloween! Next!" DJ said to the trick-or-treaters.

"What happened to Nebbercracker's house?" asked a familiar little girl with long pigtails. She was dressed as a princess.

"It turned into a monster, so I had to blow it up," replied DJ.

The girl nodded sagely, as if she had been sure it would come to that someday. DJ knew what she had come for.

"We need a Big Wheel!" he called down to Chowder.

Chowder looked around the mound of toys. "Big, uh, I think we're all out," he responded.

"Not on my watch," said Mr. Nebbercracker. Overjoyed to give back what the house had taken for so long, he rummaged through the pile and came up with the girl's tricycle.

"Thank you, mister," she said, flashing a big grin.

As she skipped off, Chowder and Mr. Nebbercracker climbed out of the hole with more toys.

HONK HONK!

"There's my mom," Jenny said as a big luxury car pulled up. "We should hang out again . . . soon."

"Yes," DJ and Chowder said at the same time. Jenny laughed and leaned in to hug the two boys before climbing into the car.

"She grabbed my butt," Chowder said as Jenny's car drove away.

"That's nice, Chowder," DJ said.

DJ turned back to Mr. Nebbercracker, who was

still handing out toys. "Hey, Mr. Nebbercracker," he said, "it's time to go."

"You go on. I've got some work to do." He threw Chowder his basketball.

"All right, see you later!" Chowder replied.

"And stay out of trouble," said Mr. Nebbercracker.

The two boys waved at him and headed across the street.

"Think he'll be okay?" DJ asked.

"Yeah, he'll be fine. He'll go on vacation, get some color, and maybe meet someone new. Maybe this time, a nice beach house."

Walking up to DJ's driveway, DJ and Chowder were greeted with the glare of headlights. DJ's parents were home.

DJ's mom got out of the car and yelped in surprise at DJ and Chowder's dirt-smeared and battle-worn faces. "What's going on?" she asked cheerfully. "No, don't tell me! Are you . . . dirty pirates?"

DJ smiled. "That's it," answered DJ, "we're dirty pirates, Mom."

"Oh, you look adorable," she told them before heading inside. "Well, have fun tonight!"

Chowder bounced his basketball and took a shot at the hoop in the driveway. This time the ball lodged between the rim and the backboard with a thud. Maybe basketball wasn't his sport after all.

"You were right," Chowder told DJ as he looked at all the kids in the street. "We're definitely too old for trick-or-treating."

"No question about it," agreed DJ. But as he watched the trick-or-treaters get their bags filled with candy, he added, "On the other hand, we've been working all night."

"Candy time?" Chowder asked hopefully.

"Candy time," said DJ.

"We're back!" Chowder yelled excitedly, and the boys ran to join the crowd.

Moments later Bones climbed out of the basement, covered with dust, wood chips, and bits of plaster and insulation, but as alive as ever. He gazed around for a minute as if he didn't know where he was. He patted the dust off his jacket as more figures emerged from the pit where Mr. Nebbercracker's house had once stood.

It was puffy Officer Landers and his partner, Officer Lister. They clumsily pulled themselves out of the old foundation and eyed the young man suspiciously.

Bones glanced at the costumed kids and at the

dark hole in the ground. He then turned to the two police officers.

"Happy Halloween," he said to them before ambling off.

The officers nodded, Lister still looking like he might yell "Freeze" at any moment. "You too," Landers replied, flicking a piece of debris from his uniform. "Happy Halloween."